The #ActuallyAutistic Guide to Building Independence

from the author

The #ActuallyAutistic Guide to Advocacy
Step-by-Step Advice on How to Ally and Speak Up
with Autistic People and the Autism Community
Jennifer Brunton Ph.D. and Jenna Gensic
ISBN 978 1 78775 973 2
eISBN 978 1 78775 974 9

of related interest

So, I'm Autistic
An Introduction to Autism for Young Adults and Late
Teens *Sarah O'Brien*
ISBN 978 1 83997 226 3
eISBN 978 1 83997 227 0

The #ActuallyAutistic Guide to Building Independence

Practical, Step-by-Step Advice for
Teens, Young Adults, and Those
Who Care About Them

**Jennifer Brunton, Ph.D.
and Jenna Gensic M.A.**

Jessica Kingsley Publishers
London and Philadelphia

First published in Great Britain in 2025 by Jessica Kingsley Publishers
An imprint of John Murray Press

1

A CIP catalogue record for this title is available from the
British Library and the Library of Congress

ISBN 978 1 80501 000 5
eISBN 978 1 80501 001 2

Printed and bound in the United States by Integrated Books International

Jessica Kingsley Publishers' policy is to use papers that are natural,
renewable and recyclable products and made from wood grown in
sustainable forests. The logging and manufacturing processes are expected
to conform to the environmental regulations of the country of origin.

Jessica Kingsley Publishers
Carmelite House
50 Victoria Embankment
London EC4Y 0DZ

www.jkp.com

John Murray Press
Part of Hodder & Stoughton Ltd
An Hachette Company

The authorised representative in the EEA is Hachette Ireland, 8 Castlecourt Centre,
Castleknock Road, Castleknock, Dublin 15, D15 YF6A, Ireland.

Contents

Stage Two: Advocating for Inclusive Transitions to Adulthood

Stage Three: Advocating for More Inclusive Workplaces and Communities

Introduction

What I find challenging about transitioning into young adult-hood is how high the expectations are... It feels like...society expects you to conform, get a job, be independent, grow up fast, and suck it up. I don't think that's realistic.

—ANONYMOUS (SHE/HER)

Context

Our first book, *The #ActuallyAutistic Guide to Advocacy: Step-by-Step Advice on How to Ally and Speak Up with Autistic People and the Autism Community*, was meant for everybody. We were both raising families while doing the writing and research, and we were watching the Autistic people and neurodiverse families we knew struggle with a range of challenges arising from living in a world designed for neurotypicals. We believed there was lots of room along the whole lifespan and in all areas of interaction for more input from Autistic voices!

From our own experience, though, we started to suspect that the transitions involved in shifting to young adult-hood—however that evolution might look for any specific person—were perhaps the trickiest time of life for young Autistic people.

At the time this book was conceived, Jenny was witnessing her son's transition out of high school and was shocked by the comparative lack of available community and support resources for Autistic young adults. The organizations that did exist were overburdened, and public perceptions of Autistic adulthood, while evolving, were sometimes dismissive or demeaning. While the public school system certainly had its pitfalls, the wider world did not seem at all as welcoming or encouraging as she would have hoped, and she wondered how her son would find his way. She recalled her own years of trying—with mixed results—to navigate the worlds of higher education and work as she sought to live independently.

Jenna had a son in middle school, with the high school transition looming. Her family was questioning everything, from how to approach course selections and map out a daily class schedule that conserved energy throughout the school day, to considering appropriate job opportunities, and trying to find an extracurricular niche he'd reap the benefit of for years to come.

For a variety of reasons, the journey to increased independence and adulthood—again, in whatever form that might take for each person—tends to hold unique challenges for neurodivergent people. We may build our autonomy on a variable timeline, in different ways, and/or relying on atypical types of connections and help. (Everyone needs help! We will talk more about this later.) As we each take that unique journey, we also have much to offer along the way. Kmarie (prefers not to use pronouns) states this beautifully:

> As an autistic person, the line between dependence and independence is often quite different from a neurotypical person. Instead of being ashamed or feeling less-than when I need my community, I now know I bring worth and value to theirs as well. I wish I would have embraced interdependence earlier in my journey than I did. Life is more fluid and less stressful this way.

Increased autism awareness and earlier diagnoses have offered today's teens and young adults an advantage of self-awareness the generation before them didn't have access to. Now, Autistic advocates who have spoken about these particular teen and young adult transitions based on their unique, intimate expertise are guiding Autistic youth and their families, teachers, caregivers, partners, therapists, friends, and other allies and advocates to build a strong foundation of understanding and acceptance.

During the early planning stages of this book, we were approached by an Autistic advocate from *Detester Magazine* for assistance distributing a petition that included experiences from Autistic teens and young adults, calling for greater inclusion in schools. *Detester Magazine* is a non-profit platform dedicated to inspiring BIPOC (Black, Indigenous, and People of Color) youth activism and amplifying sociopolitical issues. This petition seemed directly aligned with our new project interest, so we were delighted to partner with members of *Detester* to begin outreach that sought #ActuallyAutistic advice on teen and young adult advocacy for inclusion, with particular emphasis on the intersectionality of disability, race, and LGBTQIA+ (lesbian, gay, bisexual, transgender, queer, intersex, asexual, and other) identities.

We want to make it very clear from the outset that we, as neurodivergent people (Jenny) with proudly neurodiverse families (both), are huge believers in the inherent value, equality, rights, wholeness, and worth of all neurologies and Autistic ways of being. We don't see autism as a disorder, per se (even though it is "officially" labeled as such), never mind a disease, as some people erroneously frame it.

We do understand that almost everyone needs others—whether because of their greater knowledge, skills, or resources—throughout their journey to adulthood. While this book uses the word "independence," we know that the reality of human life rests on *interdependence*—for people of all neurologies! Along with Beecher (he/him), we encourage people to reach out: "Never be afraid to ask for help, there are always people willing to help you. Even if it doesn't always seem that way." At the same time, we do not think there is anything "wrong" with Autistic people that needs to be "fixed."

So we are not suggesting that an Autistic person should do anything at all, besides just, above all, being their own self. What we are offering—for those who are interested, whether Autistic or neurodivergent in some other way, or neurotypical—are ideas about making the world a better place for Autistic people, focusing on building independence and sourced from Autistic people themselves.

Of course, we understand that every Autistic person must form their own opinions and make their own choices about how they perceive and live their own unique selfhood. Our lives are also impacted by other Autistic people, as well as neurotypical parents, friends, teachers, partners, therapists, and so on, who may also have an influence or role to play.

But we actively oppose any attempts to "cure" autism. "Fixing" brains that work differently is a terrible idea on so many levels. People with neurodivergent brains have driven many of the greatest inventions and advances in human culture. More importantly, you absolutely do not have to be extraordinarily gifted *or* neurotypical to be of full and equal human worth.

Whoever you are, the only interventions or strategies we support are those that help *you* feel more comfortable and be more successful—based on your *own* standards, needs, and desires—in your life (which, admittedly, will generally be lived in a largely neurotypically designed and oriented world that can often be disabling to people with differences).

On the other hand, we are always pro healing and growth—and anti-judgment! Our intention is to contribute to building a world where all Autistic people can flourish as children, teens, young adults, and adults, so we respect whatever that means for any Autistic person. We are here to provide tools to help you make sure your actions are aligned with true self-respect and informed by an array of potentially useful and meaningful Autistic perspectives.

We understand that not all Autistic people share the same views on autism and how best to lead an Autistic life or how those around them can help support and facilitate healthy living. Our survey questions were open-ended to allow for a variety of responses, and we didn't exclude responses because they didn't fit an editorial agenda. Our focus was to elevate Autistic expertise on the period covering the teenage years and young adulthood, as well as on transitions toward independence and adulthood, by gathering speaking and non-speaking perspectives from a variety of different geographical areas, school, home, and job settings, and gender and racial identities.

Because we cover a lot of ground in this book, you'll notice that some advice may be geared more toward Autistic youth, while other suggestions might apply more to employers, parents, teachers, and so on (while still being potentially helpful to Autistic youth in their own advocacy). Jenny's writing often uses "we" to refer to Autistic people, while Jenna writes as an ally. In general, we've tried to address the widest possible audience while also always offering specific tips for Autistic people themselves. Thus, we hope it will be helpful to readers of all neurologies and life stages and situations as a guide to #ActuallyAutistic-affirming ways to grow.

We see genuine inclusion and awareness around neurodiversity as an urgent civil rights frontier, as crucial to the survival and thriving of Autistic people as any such struggle. Whether we are Black, female, LGBTQIA+, Autistic, or any other civil rights-ready status, when one rises, we all rise together. Therefore, readers of all neurologies and perspectives are welcome here.

Use this book to create or collaborate on a practical *and* inspiring map of life goals, strategies, hopes, and dreams to help with direction, motivation, and focus on your journey. You can try any and all tools that work—writing, video or voice recording, drawing, conversation, making charts or lists, and so on—to envision this map.

Our free *Discussion Guide* can also help. You can find it (along with a guide for our first book and other resources) on the Jessica Kingsley website. As an additional free online resource, we have created a substantial supplement to this text for Autistic teens, young adults, adults, and those who care about them to take their research, advocacy, and activism to another level. *Stage Four* digs deeper into shifting cultural norms, working for political and systemic evolution, and advocating for change. You can access this empowering resource on the Jessica Kingsley website.

As you'll see from our survey responses, Autistic teens and young adults are facing a lot of challenges and experiencing painful emotions from living with people and in environments that are not fully welcoming. As upsetting (and, in many cases, relatable) as these responses can be to read and think about, these young voices deserve and need to be heard—for all our sakes. We are so grateful to our respondents for their courage and honesty, and we are honored to have the opportunity to center and amplify their experiences.

You may find some of the material they (and we) share hard to process or take in—perhaps especially if it feels familiar—but these are very real experiences that demonstrate how far we still have to go in our journey to a truly inclusive world that honors all neurologies. Please take good care of yourself as you absorb this crucial information.

It is our very sincere hope that this book will build wisdom and awareness in ways that will ultimately render those challenging people and environments more welcoming. Often our respondents expressed that they want to be seen and respected by those around them as equal and valuable human beings with their own visions of independence—as much as or even more than they care about achieving any of the practical details we explore. We thus hope this book will help Autistic youth, who often feel isolated or misunderstood, feel connected, seen, and understood by their peers. And we hope it will inform and enlighten those who care about these young people, too—again, to decrease the unfair difficulties faced by Autistic youth today.

You'll also read lots of responses that are hopeful, innovative, proud, accepting, aware, strong, and happy. We want to amplify these voices and experiences, too! Many survey participants expressed both positive and negative feelings about growing up and making their way in the world as a young Autistic person.

This mix feels natural to us. After all, we are a diverse group of people with diverse emotions and experiences. Sometimes we are grateful, expect good things, and feel joy about life; sometimes we're sad, confused, lonely, mad as heck, and yearning and acting for change... This book is designed to give you tools for whatever state you're in, whether you want to celebrate or fight for justice, make connections, or carve out your own space to thrive, just read a book or educate others—or all of these.

Welcome.

About us

We'd like to start by introducing the team behind *The #ActuallyAutistic Guide to Teen and Young Adult Advocacy and Activism*. This book was a labor of love for the two writers, but we also had major input from a fabulous young collaborator and her allies, not to mention our survey respondents.

Jenny (she/they)

Hi, I'm Jennifer Brunton, Ph.D., "Dr. B" to my students, plain old "Mom" to my kids, and Jenny to my friends and family. I realized I was Autistic when I was in my twenties (I wasn't diagnosed until my late-thirties). Before that, I just thought I was weird. Because I came across mostly as cis-female and book smart, I "passed" pretty well in some ways, but always felt confused about how to "act" in any unfamiliar or intense situation, as well as in certain settings, particularly institutional or corporate contexts where I just did not get "the rules."

When I first learned about autism, I finally felt I understood my own brain and way of being. Still, it took another decade or so for me to start feeling comfortable with myself and even proud. Autism awareness when I was growing up was nothing like it is now, and I pretty much had to figure out how to sort of "fit in" and feel good about myself on my own. I always had the feeling that I had to learn everything the hard way, and would watch others navigate school and work dynamics in ways that seemed alien, wrong, incomprehensible, and unattainable to me. Because of that, I made a lot of mistakes. So one big reason I wanted to write this book was to help others avoid going through what I went through, wherever possible!

I have a son who is in his early twenties now. He's the other personal reason I wanted to write this book, along with all the other wonderful Autistic teens and young adults I know and those around the world I have yet to meet. Together, we can make the world a better place for Autistic people!

I don't think empathy and inclusion should only arise because you "know" an Autistic person or Black person or differently abled person or female person or trans person or... I love the way communities are evolving their efforts away from autism awareness and toward autism *acceptance*. Because why should you have to know about the (neurological, sexual, ethnic, etc.) details of my being to accept me—am I right?

But sometimes identifying with or being close with people in a particular group will spark additional interest in making the world a better place for them, and thereby for everyone. With a large proportion of my families of origin and orientation and closest friends being people of color and/or queer, and as I grew up partly in Panama as one of two white people for hundreds of miles, BIPOC and LGBTQIA+ Autistic teens and young adults have a particularly central place in my advocacy and activism. For this book, Jenna and I explicitly sought to amplify voices from these demographics, as well as other marginalized groups, and will continue to advocate in this area in any way we can.

Jenna (she/her)

Hello Reader, I'm so pleased you've chosen to explore these pages! I'm a neurotypical mother of four, first introduced to autism about 23 years ago when one of my younger brothers was diagnosed (he was 13). I had a surface-level understanding of his struggles throughout middle and high school, all through the eyes of an older sibling. I spent a brief amount of time learning about autism in college while obtaining an education degree, and then continued the learning journey seven years later, after my first son was diagnosed.

I started on the typical neurotypical parent journey, trying to learn as much as possible from doctors and writers who had studied autism—none of whom identified as Autistic. A few years into this journey, I was overwhelmed by all of the advice (often contradictory and always forceful). At the time, I was also taking graduate writing classes and studying the personal essay specifically. I loved this form of writing, appreciating its intimacy and potency, which inspired me to reach out directly to the Autistic community in search of better advice for my son.

I've learned a lot through this process that I'm certain I couldn't have gained from non-Autistic experts. I've also found a network of work partners and friends. Most importantly, I'm learning how to help my Autistic son have confidence in his Autistic identity and a positive self-concept. My learning process could best be described as a crawl—learning a few things here and there that I continually piece together to offer my son (and adult brother) a more inclusive, accepting world. But I believe that a commitment to continual change (no matter how small the "Aha! moment" is) matters, and that staying grounded in Autistic expertise will keep the world headed in the right direction.

I was especially excited to be a part of this project because it incorporates a variety of different responses from a variety of different identities and focuses on a critical (and sometimes overlooked) life period of transitions and growth. I have an Autistic teenager, and I'm excited about how this book will inform his current and future teachers and employers.

We, Jenna and Jenny, collaborated with the wonderful teens and young adults of *Detester Magazine* to design our survey for this book, and to get it out there into the world. Here's a little bit about them.

Siyu/Suzanna (she/they)

Hello! My name is Siyu (Suzanna) Chen. I am an Autistic self-advocate and a current undergraduate student at University College London (UCL). Growing up as an Asian cis-female, my Autistic traits were buried under layers of misunderstanding and dismissal under a narrow and stigmatizing diagnostic system, especially so in East Asian cultures. This led to intense insecurities about myself and other mental health concerns. But even after my late diagnosis at 18, my hope of being finally accepted as who I have always been was shattered by the reality that we still have a long way to go to accept autism as a beautiful difference—again, especially in non-white cultures.

With my turbulent teenage years not far behind me, I believe promoting autism acceptance for both my fellow autistic young adults and their non-autistic peers would help establish the self-confidence we need as we step further into societies not built for us. As a member of *Detester Magazine*, I hope my contribution to this book can help Autistic teens and young adults, especially those with other minority identities, to recognize the value of their voice, the validity of their differences, and the need and means to self-advocate for the acceptance we are all entitled to.

In gratitude for all the help we've received along the way from the #ActuallyAutistic community, and to further our goals of Autistic wellness, inclusion, justice, and progress, Jenny and Jenna will be donating 10 percent of the royalties from this book to the organization chosen by Siyu: The Autistic People of Color Fund (https:// autismandrace.com).

About our respondents

Of course, this book was shaped above all by the contributions of the more than 100 Autistic teens, young adults, and adults who completed our survey and/or gave us permission to quote from interviews on Jenna's blog, as well as from Jenny and Jenna's personal correspondences.

We are happy to report that our #ActuallyAutistic respondents are genuinely diverse in many, many ways, from nationality to gender identity to ethnicity. Roughly 30 percent, or about one-third, of our respondents are people of color, representing African, Asian, and Indigenous descent. While the majority hail from the United States, we also had significant responses from Canada, Europe, the United Kingdom, Asia, Australia, and New Zealand, with South Africa and Israel in the mix as well.

While we did not include questions around gender identity or sexuality, many respondents identified as and discussed being LGBTQIA+. Many also referred often to the activism and solace found within their intersectional LGBTQIA+ communities.

Our respondent sample was inevitably weighted toward currently verbal people, including non-speaking people who use AAC devices. Our survey parameters initially comprised only teen and young adult Autistics, including those who are self-diagnosed. However, we found, not surprisingly, that Autistic people of various ages had much to share on the subject of transitioning to independence and adulthood. We've included those perspectives as well.

We refer to most participants by their last name. When

only one name was given on the survey, we use that one. We also honor respondents who requested anonymity by not revealing their name or identifying details. Additionally we've also selectively anonymized quotes that may have identified people who did not participate in the survey.

For all of our collected #ActuallyAutistic insights, we retained the preferred pronouns (please see below), terms, and capitalization style of each participant when quoting them, but have edited some responses for basic grammar and spelling.

About our survey

We began our survey outreach with a long survey, encompassing about 30 questions. Suzanna worked with *Self Advocates United as 1* to develop an accessible language prototype for the survey to ensure greater access. Since not everyone has the time, energy, desire, or capacity to answer such a long series of questions, we then developed a shorter survey with just four questions.

Our surveys included consent forms that explained how participant responses would be used. If a participant filled out the survey, but did not complete a consent form, we used their content and maintained anonymity. We have included the texts from both our long- and short-form surveys in Appendix A, as well as a contributor list of those who wished to include their names/contacts in Appendix B (some of these people chose not to have their names linked with their survey responses when quoted in the text).

The combination of so many surveys and interviews from a truly varied cross-section of the world provided rich content and key insights for Autistic teens, young adults, and adults finding their way in the world, as well as for building more inclusive schools, workplaces, and communities.

Goals

We wanted to offer encouraging, empowering, actionable ideas and personal perspectives, primarily by amplifying the experiences and insights of #ActuallyAutistic teens and young adults, with some input from older Autistic people reflecting on their earlier years. Our work is dedicated to Autistic mental, physical, social, and emotional wellness, and inclusion, justice, and progress.

True community and connection are also primary goals. We believe that having access to a wide range of Autistic voices reduces isolation and misinformation while contributing to the empowerment and overall wellness of Autistic people everywhere.

Similarly, positive, genuine, lasting change is a central aim. We believe that when Autistic people themselves lead the way, and others (including those in power and with certain privileges) actively listen and learn, real change can happen. Acknowledging past and current injustices can be instructive for future behavior, but it also can be an important aspect of respecting someone's whole identity and to being a decent human being. Talking about broken systems, marginalization, racism, sexism, ableism, and so on does not perpetuate these struggles, but rather promotes healing and progress.

Language and terms

Let's face it, it's hard to get language and terms right all the time. But it's worth the effort, because it can really hurt when we don't. When Jenna was first corrected by an Autistic advocate for the language she was using around autism, she immediately wanted to learn all the common language mistakes people made and how she was supposed to speak about autism. She was focusing on behavior change, rather than mindset. However, she realized that the commitment to making positive behavior changes opened the doors to engagement in the right conversations that eventually led to critical mindset change. Mindset shifts come with repeated exposure, a commitment to continual learning, and respecting Autistic expertise—and using the right language is a great way to start.

Many readers will not be surprised when we say that people who should know better sometimes speak or write using words that are outdated, insensitive, or inappropriate. That includes everyone—from teachers to parents to peers, even fellow Autistics. Both of us definitely had a lot of people and places we wanted to share our first book about autism advocacy with for this reason alone!

Even those of us who think we have it "right" can mess up. Language is always evolving, and we are always learning. Also, different people prefer different words, so that can get confusing. Wherever possible, we use the words and capitalization preferences (autistic/Autistic) that people themselves prefer.

In short, language is important, which is why we consciously and continually strive to make language choices that are broadly inclusive and respectful, as well as autism- and disability-affirming. We will do our best to acknowledge areas of difference, explain language choices, and always defer to individual preferences when quoting particular sources.

Here are some terms we use in the book, with explanations of what we mean when we use them.

Activism

The words "advocacy" and "activism" refer to similar things. Activism entails advocating for a better world. How is autism activism different from autism advocacy? For one thing, it is more about the political and social aspects of being Autistic in the world. According to Dictionary.com, activism refers to "the doctrine or practice of vigorous action or involvement as a means of achieving political or other goals." So an autism activist might march for Autistic rights, stage protests or demonstrations to raise awareness of neurodiversity, or write letters or emails or make calls to teachers, administrators, business owners, or politicians to demand change.

Another distinction is that the word "activism" also usually refers to calling for change, whereas advocacy may often involve making sure that the rules designed to protect people of all neurologies and abilities and disabled people and Autistic people are being honored in the way most inclusive to an Autistic person or Autistic people.

Activism furthers transformation and evolution on a local, community, national, and global scale, rather than advocating for personal success, progress, and inclusion. But many people use these words interchangeably—and that's fine, too. (For more on this, please see Stage Four, our online resource on the Jessica Kingsley website, which takes a deep dive into activism.)

Advocacy and self-advocacy

Early on in our writing of this book, we received a communication from someone who was very concerned with our use of the term "self-advocacy." They felt that we were implying that self-advocacy was the only valuable or necessary sort, or that everybody should self-advocate. We didn't mean either of these things, so we'd like to clarify the different types of advocacy we are presenting.

Yes, self-advocacy in this context refers to an Autistic person advocating for themselves. But when we use the term, we intend it in an empowering, respectful sense. In no way is it meant to imply that all Autistic people should or can advocate for themselves, or that self-advocacy should or can be the only type. Inclusion means consideration and involvement from all parties.

Advocacy itself can mean people (Autistic or not) who are specifically advocating for an(other) Autistic person or persons. It can even refer to people (Autistic or not) reading our books or other Autistic source materials to encounter a multiplicity of Autistic voices to guide their advocacy and build their own awareness.

Age

What do we mean by teens and young adults? One aspect of autism many Autistic people experience is developmental differences. Jenny is still learning to be an adult—at what many people might consider a very advanced age for such an activity. Although her teen and young adult kids don't believe her, she was once a teenager herself. Moreover, she was an Autistic teen and young adult. Frankly, she struggled with the rules, customs, and attitudes of the neurotypical world. Many of these did not make sense to her, others seemed immoral. And she surely missed others entirely. She went to three middle schools and three high schools (one twice). During high school, she ran away for a year. Academics and executive function came easily to her in her particular neurology, but social subtleties did not. Even then, like many Autistic people, Jenny lacked a certain amount of respect for authority and hierarchy. She said things that, in retrospect, probably worked against her, and probably regularly missed opportunities to further her own interests. She was never quite able to fit in or get ahead as much as her efforts should have enabled her to do. This affected her in every institution she was a part of, from elementary school to her graduate studies at Columbia University, from which she ultimately earned a doctorate. Subsequently, she has probably had about ten careers, from novelist to professor to yoga teacher.

The point is, despite a lot of really strong strengths, it took Jenny a really long time to figure out the neurotypical world at all. So she is a good example of the transition from childhood and young teenagehood to young and then full adulthood taking a developmentally different course. And while those transitions vary widely for Autistic people, it's fairly common for many aspects of them to be more challenging and longer lasting than they are for neurotypical people.

Our shared #ActuallyAutistic insights about navigating these life shifts, however, can make a huge difference in Autistic lives and in society itself. These perspectives can offer calm in times of transitional anxiety, and hope amid despair at any stage of life. They also can awaken communities and the world to the need for systemic, inclusive change.

But back to the issue of age. We've chosen to write about teenagers and young adults because of the crucial role these years (decades) play in Autistic peoples' lives. Bottom line, though, we think a reasonable age range for this subject matter spans the early teen years to...the age of anyone "still figuring it out." Because Autistic people often see age differently, we are a bit more age-agnostic as to exactly what constitutes the many elements of transitions to adulthood. However, the majority of our survey respondents were teens and young adults.

Allyship

Allyship is related to advocacy, and, in this context, usually refers to a neurotypical person who is closely allied with an Autistic person or persons. We use the term when there is a clear, deep, and mutual alignment in which the ally is actively embraced by the Autistic person or persons as such.

Neurotypical people should be careful not to call themselves allies. Their validation comes from the Autistic community, and they must understand that the leading voice in the conversation on autism must come from Autistic people. They should constantly strive to be allies, but be humble enough to recognize that the title isn't theirs to claim. In *Demystifying Disability*, Emily Ladau explains that "ally" isn't an official title. "Simply saying 'I'm an ally to the XYZ-marginalized community' isn't how allyship works. In fact, being an ally is really more of a 'show, don't tell' kind of thing" (2021, p.141).

Helplessness and being in need of help are common stereotypes associated with disability, and recognizing that the disability community isn't in constant need of saving is an important first step to being an ally (Ladau, 2021, p.142). Ladau instead asserts that disabled people are "in need of a world that recognizes our rights and our humanity without question" (p.142). Strong allyship encourages piercing scrutiny of the world, constantly seeking and advocating for changes to obvious and immediate inclusion and access barriers, as well as broader systemic obstacles. This can occur both in small-scale efforts within one's own home as well as large-scale regional or national activism. And allyship doesn't come quickly or easily. Allies keep making mistakes and keep working to do better: "Being an ally needs to be an ongoing process" (Ladau, 2021, p.143).

Recent use of the word "accomplice" fills a similar role, with the implication that an accomplice is willing to put themselves on the line with their marginalized peer(s) to achieve certain political, social, or personal justice outcomes.

Intersectionality

In a nutshell, this term refers to the overlapping nature of differences and the ways our identities can be empowering and/or oppressing. But it also points to how we can all uplift one another—and how when we do so, we are in truth also uplifting ourselves. The concept originated in Black and queer communities seeking to express and confront their own marginalization, and has grown to embrace other elements of identity, including religion, gender, sex, race, ethnicity, nationality, class, sexuality, disability, physical appearance, neurodiversity, and more.

Justice

In our view, justice involves not just equality but equity. That means not just that people are treated equally, but that they have the same opportunities—to live full lives, work, build relationships, strive for independence, and make their own choices.

Genuine justice isn't merely about tolerance or awareness.

It entails *active* inclusion and belonging. For ourselves and our loved ones, and for this world we live in, we want our work to build justice for people of all neurologies.

We believe really taking in and digesting others' voices nurtures the basic human interconnections that enable all of us to offer the same respect and consideration to all people. When people who are willing and able to work for change—ideally, including those in power—are part of this deep listening process, progress is inevitable. Progress toward just laws and societies then makes space for everyone to succeed in their own ways. In short, justice allows people to function on a level playing field. (See Stage Four, our online resource on the Jessica Kingsley website, for extensive information about societal, cultural, and political justice and change.)

Neurodivergent (ND) and neurotypical (NT)

In our previous book, we used "neurodivergent/ND" to refer to Autistic people. Although we have been mindful all along that the term also encompasses other neurologies, including attention deficit hyperactivity disorder (ADHD) and bipolar disorder, we've subsequently become aware that using this term in that way can leave out those populations. While we will continue to use "neurotypical/NT" to discuss non-neuro-divergent people, in this book, we will mostly avoid using ND when referring only to Autistic people. Nonetheless, our work inherently relies on the words of others, and we always use the original language of each respondent, so several instances of this term to refer to Autistic people remain.

Pronouns

People's pronouns (she/her, she/they, he/him, he/they, they/them, e/em/eir) represent an important aspect of their identity. We affirm and use the pronouns of each person mentioned and/or quoted in this book. For respondents who did not share their pronouns, we use "(NP)" to indicate that status, and refer to them as "they/them." When quoting respondents anonymously, we have retained their pronouns in parentheses.

Advocating for More Inclusive Homes and Schools

Our research reveals some of the key things that Autistic teens and young adults really want and truly need. We believe their insights can be incredibly useful in helping shape advocacy and activism (whether for yourself or others) around progress that will genuinely improve conditions for Autistic youth and adults during key phases of their lives. Of course, many readers will have their own opinions, wants, and needs—and we are aware of and respect all such differences and choices.

We found that there were several aspects of life in which respondents repeatedly called for change. That's because elements of these contexts were invariably somehow disabling for many Autistic people. Therefore, a big part of our advocacy and allyship work will inherently involve finding ways to evolve these limiting and debilitating situations or phenomena into genuinely positive, inclusive ones. In every section and question of the survey, people discussed challenges with these factors:

- Relationships
- Cultures
- Policy and laws
- Environments, including built/material and institutional contexts.

Respondents also suggested strategies and tools to address these challenges.

In Stage One, we start at home, the place where most people grow a fundamental sense of belonging, stability, and confidence. We then move on to schools, the highly impactful social and educational matrix of the teen years. In both settings, we grapple with tweaking the above four factors to generate real inclusion and progress for Autistic young people.

Foster Inclusive, Accepting Family Dynamics and Homes

I think that living with my parents is hard because they don't exactly understand the extent of my disabilities.

—CORDEIRO (THEY/THEM)

Home routines, dynamics, schedules, and rules vary widely among families, but healthy homes all offer a place to learn and grow and thrive. This doesn't mean that these spaces are devoid of conflict. However, healthy homes manage conflict in ways that promote growth and still offer a place of respite for those who need to avoid conflict or simply recharge. This step reveals how autism acceptance and advocacy can take root in the home, thereby providing essential self-esteem and confidence, along with a safe and nurturing base from which to navigate important transitions.

We heard again and again that having someone (or more than one person) in your corner who truly listens to, supports, uplifts, and believes in you can make all the difference. But what are some practical ways to make sure this happens at home? Autistic teens and young adults and those who care about them will find below seven concrete ways that family and home dynamics can be proactively improved, ideally by all parties concerned. And families and others can learn more about how giving Autistic youth a voice and trusting them to communicate what they need will enable families, loved ones, and any relevant people to better support them by co-creating autism-friendly home environments.

Fostering inclusive homes, No. 1: Understand that all young people need a refuge

Why is this needed?

We all need rest. Downtime. And we need a safe space to recover. Because daily work, school, social, and health environments, commitments, and routines are often designed by and for neurotypicals, spending time in safe, affirming spaces is especially critical for Autistic people. Even with the many dedicated NT and Autistic advocates hard at work to improve autism awareness, acceptance, and accessibility, it's impossible to shelter ourselves or the people we care about from every daily life challenge out in the larger world. Allowing your home to be a refuge creates a safety net for when life gets tiring or completely overwhelming.

Many Autistic people have stressed the benefits of having a safe home, and also warned of the devastating impact that occurs when they aren't granted a daily refuge. Families, loved ones, and Autistic youth seeking to improve home environments, and Autistic young adults transitioning to creating (or looking to improve) their own home spaces, can integrate the elements set out below into their efforts.

Avoiding forcing social norms

One way to make your home feel more comfortable and safe is to relax an emphasis on NT social norms. Autistic people feel public pressure to adhere to social norms (often in more intense and exhausting ways than NTs do) every time they leave the house, so it's crucial to have a space to relieve that pressure. One survey contributor says they wish their family would stop "forcing social 'norms'" and accept "different ways of being." Conversely, Conrad (he/him) says that while outside the home his shy nature made him a target, eliciting advice for him to "open up" more, he appreciated how he never felt that pressure at home. "I think they [my family] understood me—'well, he's one of those, that's all'—and left me alone. My brothers were the same—I never felt pressured at home and I was happy there."

Creating space for rest and recuperation

Differences can make Autistic youth the targets of abuse in schools and other public spaces, often forcing them to attempt to mask in order to fit in or avoid mistreatment. Being marginalized/bullied and masking are draining and painful. Therefore, having a stress- and trauma-free retreat becomes essential for survival. Sankar (he/him) explains that the pressure to be as neurotypical as possible increased after he learned to Spell to Communicate:

> In its kindness in recognizing me as thinking and intelligent, the world failed to accept the way my body regulates itself. This autistic way of regulation, in our world, implies a lack of intelligence. This way of assessing intelligence needs to end now.

A welcoming home contributes to self-regulation, honors multiple intelligences and modes of self-expression, and enables Autistic people to simply *be themselves*.

Discomfort in certain social settings and experiencing pressure to mask are consistent among most Autistic people in a variety of different situations. Running (she/her) says she trusts her neurodivergent children to recognize when life is too challenging or overwhelming for them. When they communicate that they have reached "peak saturation," Running says she gives them space to "rest and recuperate." "I only make demands of them when they are capable of meeting those demands. Pushing an overwhelmed, autistic child because adults want more just leads to shutdown or meltdown, and that isn't beneficial for anyone." Running also stresses the importance of adapting the home to allow for fortifying rest:

> No one can rest properly if there is a perpetual something that triggers sensory discomfort. For my family, this means plain decoration, minimizing strong smells, having quiet spaces, having spaces to bounce, and having a plethora of fiddle toys. All of these things help us to self-regulate, so we can then function better within the often chaotic outside world.

While creating sensory and emotional refuge will mean different things for different people, doing so is always a fundamental element of an inclusive home.

Fostering inclusive homes, No. 2: Avoid generalization about "life skills" and what it takes to be "successful"

Why is this needed?
The adults in our lives naturally have more experience navigating the world and thus tend to share advice on how to best handle what life throws at us. Adults and other influencers have a responsibility to use their experience to help steer Autistic youth in what they truly believe is the "right" direction, but should also understand that standards and expectations that were helpful for their own healthy development or success (defined however they wish) may not be necessary for others. Further, overemphasizing some "life skills" that Autistic youth may struggle with can be detrimental to their self-worth.

Success can be defined in many different ways, and a culture's idolizing of certain types of success can lead to a person's value being judged by their usefulness or productivity. This puts marginalized people at a tremendous disadvantage given the inequitable world we live in. It deprives many Autistic people (among others) of opportunities to shape their own valid notions of what's important, and makes it less likely that their activities will be supported or valued. These skewed standards also make it hard for them to feel good about their lives and accomplishments.

An autism-affirming home makes room for evolving and inclusive ideas around success and key life skills. This more nuanced perspective on success is related to the idea of avoiding assumptions that the parent/teacher/therapist agenda is "best," a topic we discussed at length in our first book.

Considering why you are emphasizing certain skills

Kitten (she/her) explains that many adults speak generally about the importance of "life skills" with children and have expectations they would never demand from adults. Kitten offers examples of children only being able to eat foods that others choose for them, waiting for permission to use the bathroom, or wearing undergarments that are chosen by someone else. Autistic teens and young adults often feel like those around them want them to conform to these types of expectations or develop particular skills, even when they themselves aren't interested or ready. Kitten explains that in most contexts of adult life, people have a lot more freedom than children and more marginalized adults, who may still be pressured by people in their lives to "perform" in certain ways. "Reading and writing are also examples," Kitten notes. "It's extremely useful to be able to read and write, but I've known successful university students who couldn't do one or both of those things."

Understanding that "age appropriate" isn't always a reliable or useful standard

Some families also try to encourage socialization or public outings they deem "appropriate" or "typical" at different ages and may discourage interests that others might view as "childish." Many of the Autistic youth we heard from prefer to follow their own developmental journey. One respondent (she/they) explains that her parents try to take her to places that are "age-appropriate" or try to convince her to go to "age-appropriate" events, like parties. "I understand that they're trying to make my life as normal as possible, but I don't think that my life has to be normal, as long as I enjoy it." Not only are age-appropriate references usually based on neurotypical standards and therefore inaccurate comparisons, they also tend to normalize NT age-appropriate development as "good" and anything else as "bad," thus casting judgments on what should be neutral developmental classifications. Consequently, practicing acceptance of interests and preferences without making age-related judgments is helpful for Autistic people themselves, as well as their loved ones.

Considering how high expectations are impacting you, your teen, young adult, patient, student, and so on

High expectations can demonstrate faith in someone, but overemphasizing high standards when they are currently out of reach or without offering support to reach them can be unhealthy. Several survey contributors explained that their parents placed too much emphasis on them to be academically, athletically, and socially "successful."

One respondent (they/them) explains that they grew up in a household where "school success was paramount... I was expected to have high grades (higher than I could actually manage), be athletic, and social. I was constantly put down for my failures and compared to other, 'more successful,' non-mixed Chinese kids around me..." They say that things improved when they took control over their own education goals and success indicators:

> Once I didn't have to show my report card to my mother, once I was allowed to pick the courses I wanted, and once I escaped to university and was the sole person in charge of my education, I was able to flourish. This only happened because I had good mentors who listened and supported the things I wanted to do with my life, and a therapist who was able to unravel a number of layers of abuse and trauma so I could see what healthy relationships looked like.

As Autistic people enter their teen years and beyond, many are eager to develop and work toward their own goals and visions of success. Families must determine a healthy balance of expectations, acceptance, and support, but it's necessary to include Autistic youth in helping determine that balance as often as possible.

Avoiding sheltering

Some Autistic people surveyed expressed frustration with how their parents' lack of understanding of autism led to controlling behaviors or an undue focus on researching their differences. One contributor (they/them) explains her irritation, "My mom does way too much research about every sliver of Identity I have." They say that they did everything possible to escape their "mother's clutches," staying busy with activities that kept them out of the house, working hard to apply for scholarships, and learning independent living skills. Another contributor (she/her) explains that getting a driver's license was a goal in order to escape her toxic family. Truly supportive neurodiverse homes embody mutual respect and uplift healthy efforts toward self-determination. This mindset is especially crucial in neurodiverse homes since many Autistic young people remain at home longer than their NT peers for a variety of reasons.

Fostering inclusive homes, No. 3: Embrace all identities and recognize aspects of intersectionality, including LGBTQIA+ identities, and race and ethnicity

Why is this needed?

Autistic youth need to feel accepted in their home. The outside world is often unwelcoming to neurodivergent people, and it can sometimes seem as if their surroundings aren't built for them. LGBTQIA+ and BIPOC Autistic people, populations that are generally underdiagnosed (Kiefer, 2022; Mandell *et al.*, 2009; Rodriguez, 2022), often face additional significant challenges both at home and in the outside world. The intersectionality of race, disability, gender, and other factors amounts to a complex and unique mix of experiences and needs for each Autistic teen/young adult. Acceptance at home is paramount to building healthy self-worth to combat whatever adversity they face in public!

Being accepting of different sexual and gender identities

Several survey contributors discussed the intersectionality of multiple marginalized identities, some of them struggling with a lack of acceptance over their sexual orientation, gender identity, and/or gender expression. Writer and artist Liu (she/her) explains that after she realized people at her church were homophobic, it caused her a lot of inner turmoil: "I was so desperate to be accepted that I thought suppressing my sexuality and keeping it a secret was the best thing to do." By being truly inclusive and supportive, homes and families can provide the refuge to recover from such attitudes, insights for avoiding/countering them, and the courage to retain and build self-worth.

Embracing stims

For many Autistic people, stims are a vital part of who they are. In our first book, we discussed the pressure many Autistic people feel to mask and hide their stims due to the world's negative perception of atypical behaviors and the stereotypes and judgments that follow. Autistic youth can sometimes feel even more stress in this area than adults if they live in a household where stims are discouraged both in public and at home. One respondent (she/her) says that she used to worry about how she would be perceived in public because she wasn't allowed to stim anywhere as a child:

> Part of my abuse as a child was not being allowed to stim in public or even my house because it made me look weird. Not being able to flap my hands at the grocery store would lead to severe meltdowns later at home. It took a lot of work for me to get to where I am now. I freely stim in public and just ignore the odd looks I get.

Stims communicate so many different things—excitement, pleasure, stress, overwhelm, efforts to organize thoughts or process information, and more. Discouraging stims due to potential social awkwardness puts Autistic people at an incredible communication and processing disadvantage. Autistic young people themselves, and perhaps especially their families and loved ones, must consider whether they sometimes prioritize neurotypical social comfort over Autistic communication and emotional regulation. If so, we suggest shifting this mindset, starting at home.

Learning about racism

Several contributors discussed the struggle of living with racist and discriminatory parents and families. This sparks a desire for freedom in order to escape constant judgment and emotional abuse. Contributors described abusive families, racist ideologies, and families not being supportive of immigrant friends. One respondent describes how her family was concerned about appearances—praising her publicly, but treating her horribly at home because of her differences. She didn't introduce her friends to her parents because, she says, their racism and other negative qualities made them "utter disappointments." Her father mocks the Chinese language and, she says, "It's so terrifying because some of my best friends are Chinese and I hesitate to introduce them to my dad, especially because this is how he is."

Racism prevents families from bonding on a united advocacy front. In the home, it actively contributes to the pain and othering of Autistic youth of all races by impacting their family and other relationships, while oppressing them and/or forcing them to bear witness to systemic oppression. Racism occurs not only in blatant jokes and slurs, but is also interwoven in unspoken ideologies and stereotypes that feed discrimination and create systems of oppression in ways that aren't always obvious to the oppressor.

All forms of discrimination, whether against Autistic people, people of color, LQBTQIA+ people, or anyone else, exacerbate othering and cause similar issues in the home. That's because discrimination seems to place one group above others while actually bringing everyone down. It's critical for Autistic youth to speak up about intolerance, and for their families and loved ones to listen to their feelings and not become overly defensive. But the onus is also on family members to be aware of the true impacts of intolerance and to work toward personal growth in any relevant areas.

Fostering inclusive homes, No. 4: Manage conflict in safe and affirming ways

Why is this needed?
All families have conflict, and the teen/young adult years can be especially challenging. Non-violent communication techniques, along with healthy conflict resolution modeled at home, can help prepare Autistic youth for managing conflict on their own. On the other hand, as some of the contributors

share, if conflict isn't managed in safe and affirming ways at home, it can create overwhelming stress that is hard to endure. This isn't surprising for families of all neurologies, but these stories remind us that building a stable home is the foundation on which other supports or advocacy efforts can grow.

Pursuing therapy to promote stable relationships

Not having good examples of how to resolve conflicts can disrupt the safe space of a home and hinder all kinds of relationships. Autism-friendly, neuro-affirming, and #ActuallyAutistic professional help can enable families to heal and communicate better. (See Stage Four, our online resource on the Jessica Kingsley website, for more information about finding such professionals.) Some contributors said they wished their parents had been in therapy or even got a divorce. "I didn't understand how to resolve conflicts," one respondent (she/her) explains. "I didn't see that very well at home either, so that didn't help." She says that the instability at home influenced her reactions to social anxiety at school. She describes herself as always on the outside, looking in, never understanding how to play well with children. Her social anxiety came out as aggression:

> What would have helped would have been if my parents had both started individual therapy and marriage therapy and if they had decided to part ways so that we could have had a safe home... Because having safety at home will make me more receptive to getting support.

She adds that pursuing therapy (play, art, music) for herself would also have been helpful in order to process the hardships she was going through.

Being wary of infantilization and criticism

Another component of building a respectful, accepting space at home is feeling as if you are valued and respected. This entails all family members demonstrating trust and confidence in everyone's abilities and human worth. Some contributors discussed how being included in an activity or asking for their input isn't enough if they are talked to like a child. Maclean (NP) explains, "Yes, they have included me, but yet again, they talk me down as if I'm a little child. They need to understand and learn that every autistic is different and not the same."

Some contributors shared frustration around being criticized for expressing their emotions and having to deal with parents yelling and deflecting their emotions back on them. Growing up, Jenny often felt criticized for feeling the "wrong" things, being "oversensitive," and "not letting go" on the timeframe that her family members (who were doing their best in a time of limited autism awareness) expected. She now knows that trying to repress these feelings led to frequent meltdowns and migraines—and that feeling understood and accepted would have soothed her and made a huge difference in her mental health in general.

Many of the Autistic youth we heard from discussed how they want to be treated fairly and would prefer their feelings and opinions to be seen as valid and worthy of attention. Parents and family members can strive to create a safe space for participation and self-expression by demonstrating faith in their Autistic family members and helping them learn to cope with conflict.

Fostering inclusive homes, No. 5: Integrate all family members in activities and respect their needs

Why is this needed?

Accepting all family members and respecting their needs seems like an obvious, basic life rule, but inclusion and acceptance aren't simple when needs, interests, and lifestyles vary. Autistic people often want to be integrated in formal and informal familial activities, as long as their needs are respected and supported. But most of all, they want to feel loved and accepted, which is of utmost importance in a world that sometimes isn't very kind to them.

Making sure everyone feels wanted and included

Autistic youth want to feel comfortable in their homes. This means a variety of different things. It not only means that they feel safe, but that they also feel wanted, included, and that their needs aren't too much work for their family to manage. Sankar (he/him) emphasizes the similarities Autistic people have to their non-Autistic family members, "They are beings like you with a full measure of thought, ideas, and needs playing in their soul. Souls who long to be less work for their loved ones. Souls who question their place in society." Sankar says that going directly to an Autistic person and learning about them is important, rather than faulting their neurology because of the differences. "Be an ally, go to an autistic, and work with them, not for them. Get to know an autistic non-speaker." Birch says that she feels included simply when she's "being treated like a human or someone that matters."

There are a lot of ways Autistic teens and young adults and their families can ensure that all family members feel included. Some respondents shared how making an effort to ask their input about what they need or what makes them comfortable can help. Emily (she/her), a blogger at 21andsensory, appreciates:

> ...when someone asks me what might make me feel more comfortable in an environment or if someone really listens to me when I am struggling in a situation and helps me to safely remove myself from it or brainstorm ideas of what I could do.

Others discussed the importance of talking freely about their interests and having people listen to them with genuine curiosity and attention. They want to feel listened to, not ignored or patronized.

Some people said they simply wanted their families to love them—quirks and all. Others feel loved, but their differences are still considered obstacles. Sarah (she/her) says, "Unfortunately, I grew up in an emotionally abusive household. My parents used my quirks and 'weirdness' as fodder for abuse, which only encouraged me to hide myself from the world—and them." The threat of abuse, in turn, leads to masking. Sarah continues:

> Because of that, I've battled depression for most of my life. Autistics live in a neurotypical world and having a safe space to be ourselves is necessary to our mental health. Thankfully, I've found that space with my husband... So, my wish is simple—I wish my parents had accepted and loved me, quirks, weirdness, and all. I hope parents of neurodivergent children never underestimate the value their unconditional love has in their children's ability to thrive.

Families can also be more accepting of differences, such as the need to stim, and encourage and respect varied ways of communicating. One contributor says, "Be more accepting of noticeable autistic traits like stimming and not making eye contact and using scripts in conversation." He tells people to "listen to autistic advocates to learn what skills are most helpful to teach and what accommodations work best." The same contributor also says that AAC (augmentative and alternative communication) devices should be more available for younger people and "speaking people should learn the AAC program to model it when communicating."

Practicing patience and kindness

Being patient, loving, and listening to other people's needs goes a long way. Oesterle (she/they) says:

Embrace them [Autistic people] for their need for routine and different minds. Try to understand meltdowns and not shame them. Ask why they may appear depressed and provide resources to connect to a larger autistic community if they want! Be patient and loving.

Reardon (she/her) explains that there are so many sensory activities that can be traumatic for Autistic youth. Hair brushing was this way for her. It took time, but she's found ways to manage the sensory overload:

When I was a child, having my hair brushed was incredibly distressing. Not just the tactile sensation, which is unsurprising—our heads are covered in sense receptors. But the noise of the hairbrush moving through my hair—I wasn't overreacting, my brain genuinely processes that noise as loud and threatening. And standing still to have my hair brushed, when my vestibular and proprioceptive senses were desperate for some input to let my body know where it was and what was happening, was almost impossible too. My survival response of fear and wanting to run away was proportional to my experience. These days hair brushing is not traumatic for me, but it certainly is for many people. I sit down, I brush slowly and mindfully, and I keep my hair conditioned so it is easier to brush, and I brush it myself which is far more predictable from a tactile point of view. It's unpleasant and not my favourite task, but I don't experience sensory trauma from it anymore.

Macedo (he/him) says it helps if people understand his need for extended time to complete certain tasks. His needs often fall "under the radar," and other people expect him to deliver the same way a neurotypical person would:

I have found that I take longer to perform certain tasks than most people. For example: going through emails, following verbal and written instructions when visual is the most suited, and even shoe-tying. It is something I, and perhaps others like me, am working on, but we just need a little more time.

Author/advocate Yenn Purkis (they/them) says that the reason they co-wrote *The Awesome Autistic Go-To Guide* (2020) is because "we saw a lot of deficits focus for autistic children and young people, particularly through the diagnostic process, that needed countering." They explain that:

> Autistic kids are so frequently told that they cannot achieve much, or given the idea that they are a burden, that we wanted to put something in the world which gave them more positive messages and helped them be proud to be themselves. Additionally, we wanted autistic young people to feel less isolated and have a sense of belonging.

Being kind and calm around differences fosters home environments that uplift all family members.

Fostering inclusive homes, No. 6: Consider the benefits of an early understanding of neurodivergence and how to communicate that knowledge with others

Why is this needed?
Diagnosis carries both positive and negative weight, and the process itself can be complicated, grueling, and costly. But, in the balance, most Autistic teens and young adults we surveyed felt that knowing they are Autistic gives them insights into themselves and the people and environments around them. Many wished their families had been clearer with them about neurodivergence from the outset.

At any age, people choose to disclose or not disclose their

own diagnosis for a variety of reasons. Parents/caregivers of young children must decide when, where, and how to share the diagnosis of their children with educators, therapists, family members, and others. Parents/caregivers also must decide how and when they will explain an autism diagnosis to their Autistic children themselves.

Several survey contributors stressed the importance of doing this earlier rather than later, so Autistic children and teens can better understand themselves and the world in which they live while they are growing up. That self-knowledge can also provide tools for navigating the NT world and help with getting appropriate support. And it can ensure that first steps toward independence are rooted in full self-awareness.

Attempting to obtain an early diagnosis

Many Autistic people have shared how they wished their diagnosis had come sooner. They explain that a diagnosis would have helped them understand feelings of displacement and become stronger self-advocates. Fox (she/her) adds that her school experience might have been better as a result of having a diagnosis:

> Receiving my diagnosis sooner would have helped me come to terms with my need to rest and recharge, and helped me learn not to overexert myself socially. I am also hopeful that my school would have given me the extra support I required to learn in a more comfortable environment and perhaps be more understanding when I struggled with the workload.

When families do not seek a diagnosis, some Autistic young adults may choose to pursue their own diagnostic process for reasons related to the above. Others may not. And some self-diagnosed Autistic youth may be able to generate the tools and insights they need from their own research and self-reflection.

Being transparent about diagnosis

Some parents/caregivers struggle with deciding when to tell their children about their diagnosis. Boon (she/her) says it's important to be transparent:

> They [Autistic youth] will likely know they're different, but it can be confusing if you don't know why. I know some parents decide not to tell their children, and I can see the benefit in the short term. But long term it's better to know, because then at least they can understand why some things may seem challenging to them, and it may help young children not feel like failures or that they are useless. I was way too harsh on myself by criticizing my autistic traits from childhood (though I didn't know they were autistic traits at the time) until I got my diagnosis. Since then, it's been a lot easier with self-acceptance, and having my autism recognized is the only thing that's helped with this. It's really improved my self-esteem, and I'm no longer viewing myself as a broken person.

Having a mindset that embraces differences

Another important component to making people feel accepted and included in the home setting is embracing disability and difference. Many respondents discussed the need to feel included and accepted for who they are. Some responded that they appreciated when not too much attention is drawn to their disabilities. But others stressed that specifically avoiding the topic of disability isn't wise. Cordeiro (they/them) explains:

> A lot of people think it's best to not even talk about disability. They think it's something that should be swept under the rug. They say things like "this ability" or other things that devalue our struggles. What I think is best is trying to understand the other person. It's okay to notice somebody's differences. It's okay to treat somebody differently because they're different. By this I mean you should be

aware of people's differences and try your best to accom-modate them rather than just treating them like everybody else because the whole point of disability is that they can't do things like everybody else. I feel best when a friend is reaching out to me and asking me what I need.

Welcoming home cultures aim to assess and honor the most inclusive and loving approaches to each family member's differences.

Fostering inclusive homes, No. 7: Learn about autism and trust your Autistic loved one(s)

Why is this needed?
It's clear that recognizing and embracing neurodiversity in youth is critical in raising healthy children who become healthy teens and young adults. Many respondents stressed learning about diverse neurologies as a key aspect of their own positive personal growth, but it's also very important for families to start learning about autism as soon as possible—and to try their best to understand the interests, challenges, and motivations of their children and other Autistic family members throughout their lifespan. During this learning process, trusting their Autistic family member(s) and letting them take the lead where possible is crucial.

Having a solid understanding of the concept of an "Autistic child"
Truty (she/her) says she wishes her parents had a better under-standing of autism and Autistic children:

I wish my parents had access to even the concept of "autistic child." I don't know how they would have done things differently, but they could at least have some understanding of why I was the way I was. I'm sure I was exhausting.

A lack of awareness and understanding continue to be obstacles for many, even as they move into adulthood. Several contributors shared that they want their families to be more aware of the issues Autistic teens and young adults face and be supportive of them. Another contributor emphasized the importance of recognizing and understanding neurodiversity in children, especially young girls, as early as possible.

Trusting your Autistic loved one

As we have demonstrated above, Autistic teens and young adults deeply need their home to be a refuge. When families (including, for young adults, partners) don't recognize a need for accommodation or access or can't empathize with the Autistic experience, life can be overwhelmingly unfair. Cordeiro (they/them) explains how this disconnect can be contentious:

> My family always said that I shouldn't think about why things are harder for me, I should just live my life. However, I do think life is unfair for me in some ways. I think that things are often unaccommodating and inaccessible. I think I would be further on in life if I weren't autistic.

Many Autistic people are asking their non-Autistic family members to trust them. Autistic people have intimate experience and understanding of autism as it relates to themselves—an unparalleled insider view. They ask parents/caregivers, along with other family members and loved ones, to trust them over professionals or other "experts." Boon (she/her) says her advice to her parents would be "to trust your daughter more: she knows what she's talking about rather than the professionals who say changing schools won't make much difference." She also says it's important for Autistic people to trust themselves and their pain:

I would probably say to my younger self that school is not forever, life is better on the other side, and the amount of pain you're experiencing is not normal. My needs were not recognized; I assumed that my negative experiences were ordinary. However, I now understand them to be adverse and that many of my peers had a more positive experience in education than I did.

Finally, trusting the Autistic youth in your home and/or family also means presuming competence and expressing confidence in their worth as humans while never framing them as "inspiring" to non-disabled people. Inspiration porn and presuming competence were mentioned by several youth survey contributors, and are discussed in depth in our first book.

Conclusion: Supporting inclusivity and respect in our homes

These seven approaches to neuro-affirming family and home life provide a comprehensive roadmap to creating a truly welcoming home. Families of all shapes and sizes can integrate knowledge, respect, trust, and patience to better support and uplift neurodivergent family members. In turn, Autistic youth who experience a safe and nurturing home where they feel seen, accepted, and loved will have deeper, stronger resources with which to face young adulthood.

SUMMARY GUIDANCE:
#ActuallyAutistic practical tips for home life

- Ensure that there are safe spaces at home.
- Relax expectations for social norms at home.
- Remember that age-appropriate standards aren't always relevant or useful.

- [Autistic teens/young adults/adults] Try to avoid comparing yourself or being compared with your neurotypical loved ones, and beware of an emphasis on neuronormative cultural standards of success in the home.
- [Parents/caregivers/adults] Try to avoid comparing your Autistic child or loved one to yourself (if neurotypical) or other neurotypicals in your family or outside it, and beware of emphasizing neuronormative cultural standards of success.
- Cultivate autism-affirming family values and share learning materials (such as those found in this book) that contribute to an inclusive home.
- Be open to embracing different types of identities.
- Welcome safe stimming.
- Learn about autism and seek early diagnosis. [Parents/caregivers] Communicate the diagnosis as early as possible.

REFLECTION QUESTIONS

? What kinds of spaces in your home feel welcoming/safe to Autistic people? How could you create more such environments?

? When have you prioritized neurotypical social comfort over the comfort of an Autistic person (including yourself, if relevant)? If you have, what would help you to do better?

? Does your family express support for a variety of life skills and objectives? How do you together manage goal-setting and foster progress?

? What ways do you show support of different identities,

behaviors, interests, and so on that don't match your own?

? How did your home support (or not support) neuro-divergence when you were growing up? What could you do now and in the future to make your home more neurodiversity-friendly?

Step 2

Find Sustainable Ways to Connect

Just be kind to us. Be kind to everyone, but especially to people on the spectrum, as they are often struggling more than you think.

—ANONYMOUS (SHE/HER)

Humans of all neurologies need relationships in which they find mutual respect, understanding, shared interests, fun, trust, comfort, and love. Our research has strongly affirmed that Autistic teens and young adults very much appreciate and seek such connections—even though they can be harder for people with differences to find, make, and keep. These connections may be found in the home, through work, in schools and universities, and through other activities, but they are always vital, as Phillips (NP) explains:

I'm still trying to figure it out, but I know that having a job and things that I can do outside my family while still living with my family helps me feel more independent. As I make more friends, co-workers, and peers, I feel I can spread out my dependence among them. This personally makes me feel like I have more independence because I am not relying just solely on my parents. I'm extremely extroverted and the only extrovert in my family, so I love connecting with people and learning to let them help me with things I struggle with. I don't think this is the answer for everyone, but I feel like that's what helps me to be more independent.

Facing NT norms and expectations

Relational challenges do not arise from any lack or dysfunction in Autistic people. They come from social pressures to present and behave in "typical" ways that many Autistic people find impossible to conform to, choose not to follow, or both. Since most NT people are more naturally attuned to these norms, they may be reluctant to pursue friendship or other relationships with Autistic people. As one respondent (she/her) says, "It helps if people don't have specific social expectations, and accept me for who I am."

But NT interpersonal norms and expectations do indeed impact most Autistic youth. In Cordeiro's (they/them) words, "People misunderstand me most of the time. I struggle to make friends because I am much too blunt and straightforward for most people. I also struggle to keep them." Yet they nonetheless seek and cherish relationships: "I value deep connections and most people aren't ready to make that kind of commitment with me right away, so I end up losing people who I try to form friendships with for this reason as well." Marsh (they/them) puts it succinctly, "The social element was the hell of my youth."

Aging into interpersonal ease

Fortunately, many find that it gets easier to make friends and other connections as we get older. Ierubino (he/him) notes, "As an adult, I find it usually easier to communicate with others and make friends." One respondent (she/her) was eventually able to find a "good balance of friends" after "difficulties making friends and interacting with peers" earlier in life. And Vu (he/him) explains that college was the turning point when "I finally understood how to have and maintain and build friendships." Note that some, like Forrester (any/varies), are perfectly happy with their social skills, "I don't generally find it hard to make friends or communicate."

Inventing our own standards

Challenges in making connections also arise because many Autistic people experience a preference for varied types of relationships, some of which may diverge from what mainstream/NT cultures value. From Abramowski's (she/her) perspective, "Some people expect everyone to adhere to certain behaviors and ways, and this doesn't allow for room to differ."

Looking for more

As Autistic youth and young adults grow up, they tend to increasingly seek ways to build relationships outside the family. Our research shows we can nurture and celebrate these connections for ourselves and/or the Autistic youth in our lives in several ways, so that all of us are able to eventually "find our people." It's best of all when we can simply be ourselves:

> I've always been a social butterfly. Never shy, I'd speak to ANYONE. That said, I still had moments where I wasn't on quite the same page as others... I still felt and acted younger than my age. I was occasionally teased for this, yet I didn't let it stop me from being true to myself. I continued to talk to others and be my bubbly self! (Abramowski, she/her)

Our research revealed the following eight ways to promote respectful, sustainable connections.

Connecting sustainably, No. 1: Offer/seek opportunities to make connections

Why is this needed?

Some humans find it easy to form friendships and other relationships. Others, especially many Autistic humans, need a little more effort, scaffolding, adaptations, and encouragement. Autistic youth can use a variety of strategies—sometimes with help from older or more relationship-savvy Autistics, schools, workplaces, families, and other caring people and communities—to brainstorm, create, and support environments and events that nurture healthy, inclusive, enjoyable interactions.

Nurturing emotional literacy

Vu (he/him) suggests that teaching emotional intelligence and literacy, encouraging diverse connections, and being open to further exploration are essential keys to facilitating healthy interactions:

> If there's one thing that could help, it's that I wish schools valued the importance of emotional intelligence and fostering friendships and connections between people of different backgrounds. We're all emotional beings, and we sometimes don't know how to deal with people or ourselves. By demystifying emotions and being open to discussing them, I think we can go a long way towards not just learning to understand each other, but ourselves—and not be trapped by our own prejudices and limited worldviews (i.e., tunnel vision).

Vu's wisdom naturally extends beyond just schools to other institutions, individuals, and advocates. Whether advocating for ourselves or others, we can all take steps to learn about, express, and honor the full range of feelings. Emotionally literate, accepting environments and cultures facilitate connections for all sorts of people.

Being practical

There are also practical ways to foster connections in ways that work for Autistic youth and young adults, like gathering in welcoming sensory environments, in smaller groups, or one-on-one. Making sure you/they know someone in the group is usually a good strategy, too. One respondent (she/her), for example, says she appreciates being invited to group activities, but finds them stressful if she doesn't "know enough people." Baik (she/her) prefers getting together with individual friends rather than "a larger friendship group."

Celebrating Autistic connections

Many Autistics find it easier to befriend fellow neurodivergent people. As Dr. Damian Milton explains in his "double empathy problem" (Milton, 2018), people who experience life differently—in his research, Autistic people and neurotypical people—often encounter difficulties relating to each other. And while Autistic people have often been blamed for those challenges, he contends that those difficulties *go both ways*. Our respondents agree. In one respondent's (she/her) words, "I find it easier to communicate and befriend people who are neurodivergent." Chloe (she/her) finds that sharing neurological differences is conducive to connection, "Personally, I've found it easier to make friends with other Autistic and neurodivergent people. I find communication and understanding so much easier with people similar to myself."

Connecting sustainably, No. 2: Choose respectful language and actions (avoid jokes/insults/autism stereotypes)

Why is this needed?

Without doubt, any Autistic youth or young adult has endured language and actions that demean, stereotype, and discriminate against them and their fellow Autistics. In getting to know an Autistic youth or young adult, trying to ally with or advocate for one, or as an Autistic youth yourself, making the choice to accept only positive and affirming language is empowering both personally and interpersonally.

Some kinds of inclusive language/action choices are obvious, and avoiding such degrading terms and attitudes seems basic. But there are other more subtle ways to use language to discriminate or encourage internalized ableism, such as "joking" about "not understanding sarcasm" or suggesting everyone is "a little autistic" (Bidon, she/her).

Aspiring to truly informed, inclusive choices

Other proactively respectful choices take more thought and effort. A holistic understanding of neurodiversity helps individuals, cultures, and communities promote healthy relationships between people of all neurologies. Stereotypes and ignorance, on the other hand, impede those connections. Moody (she/her) finds it harder to make friends when people "don't understand or they have stereotypes about autism already." Kimble (she/her) echoes this perspective, "It can be very challenging because not everyone understands autistic people or what it's like being autistic in a neurotypical world."

Opting for respect and inclusion doesn't just entail avoiding common insulting or outdated language: it inherently involves developing a comprehensive awareness of the many expressions of human being. This helps us interact in ways that honor the personal integrity of all Autistic people, along with their diverse means of communication and varied sensory and processing profiles.

Connecting sustainably, No. 3: Find common interests

Why is this needed?

Shared subjects of interest are a great asset to any relationship. Since Autistic people typically encounter greater barriers to friendship in neurotypical mainstream environments, and many of us enjoy rewarding deep dives into the stuff we are passionate about, connecting around mutually enjoyable activities or topics is a win-win. As Dunford (he/him) explains, finding people who are into the same things that intrigue you opens the door to genuine and lasting friendships:

> Spectrum kids are not exactly known for their exceptional social skills. But if you get them talking about something they are passionate about, then getting them to stop talking will be the only issue you've got. I was a voracious comic reader, and as soon as I found fellow fanboys, it felt like I met someone who could finally speak my language. I was always afraid of telling other kids that I liked nerdy stuff back in the day because I was afraid that they would make fun of me. Now kids live in a golden age where they can let their geek flag fly and be embraced for being a nerd instead of being mocked.

Autistic teens and young adults are often encouraged to broaden their focus, but our passions can actually be a great conduit to connection. Marsh (they/them) says, "If anything, I'd suggest family members support individual interest spikes and hope that they may lead to social opportunities." For the same reason, work—especially meaningful, interesting work, when possible—can be another potential place to make connections.

Forging communication and community

Finding at least one thing in common helps with communication and enables people to share a common community. As Abramowski (she/her) says, "While I seem to click most frequently with others who have disabilities, I can establish a rapport with just about anyone. I can find at least one thing I share in common with them, and build the relationship from there." One respondent (she/her) suggests, "If you love manga and there is not a manga club at your school or town (for adults), then make one. Create a MeetUp group if you're an adult! Join a Discord Server... Find your own kin through your love of an interest." Forrester (any/varies) points out that having "an interest in common that brings us together" can be especially conducive to the NT/ND friendships that often pose challenges to both parties.

Shared identity is another fruitful commonality, according to Bridge (they/them):

> I have non-autistic, non-disabled friends, but they're usually another identity that I share. I have a lot of queer friends and some fellow mixed Asian friends. I don't make nearly as many friends who aren't part of one of my communities. I just don't have as much in common with them and can't really talk well with them.

Connecting sustainably, No. 4: Understand potential preferences for interactions with people of different ages, genders, and so on

Why is this needed?

When it comes to interacting, a lot of the criteria the NT mainstream holds as integral to a "valid" friendship really don't matter to many Autistic people. Being the same age, or even close in age, for example, doesn't feel necessary for genuine connection. Like Forrester (any/varies), who "as a kid...related better to adults than to my peers," many Autistic people have felt more comfortable conversing with adults since they were children. This is especially true in unfamiliar or less friendly institutional settings. One respondent (she/her) says of the school setting, "I tended to socialize more with teachers and other members of staff." One respondent (she/her) says, "As a kid I struggled to connect with my peers. I had a few friends, but if ever I was in an unfamiliar environment, I would usually talk to adults."

On the other hand, some, such as one respondent (she/her), who "had more younger friends," have found children and younger teens more accepting once they reached their teen or young adult years. For Nied (she/they), this is because "I find it easier to unmask around younger people."

Likewise, a certain fluidity around gender and friendship seems common among Autistic friends, as with one respondent's (she/her) statement that she tends to have "more male friends in comparison to female." As they get older and gender norms become more apparent, Autistic teens and young adults may find themselves questioning the status quo, as Oesterle (she/they) did:

> I never felt like a "girly girl" or was interested in boys the same way. Fashion made no sense to me. It was really hard losing friends who were boys because it was weird and I couldn't be silly anymore.

These nonconforming experiences stem partly from shifting social norms and awareness, but they also can result from skeptical views of the distinctions NT society makes between people based on factors like sex, age, race, gender, and so on.

Connecting sustainably, No. 5:
Honor online and other non-face-to-face forms of interaction

Why is this needed?

Face-to-face interaction is highly valued in most NT cultures, but isn't necessarily accorded the same status by Autistic people. As mentioned above, Autistic people don't always see the same things (here, "real-world" interaction) as important. And while they can logically understand that they are supposed to follow certain rules to "earn" or "win" at friendship, romance, and so on, they can't always discern or follow those rules. And they don't always want to! As well, the rules of engagement may be clearer, simpler, and/or less important online, making interpersonal interactions potentially less awkward.

Discovering infinite possibilities

Online interactions aren't restricted to any limited local population, so the possibility for finding people to connect with—including fellow Autistics—is exponentially increased. For Marsh (they/them), this was a lifesaver: "Online socialization based on simulation gaming, railfanning, aviation, and game design is mostly what got me as far as high school." Dunford (he/him), too, found refuge in internet-based connections with fellow comic fans:

> These days there are online groups...where you can meet like-minded readers. Reading comics is fun, but when you finish, the first thing you want to do is talk about it with someone. It doesn't do a whole lot of good to keep it to yourself, especially when you can chat about it with someone.

It's also sometimes easier from a sensory aspect to interact through a screen. As one respondent (she/they) explains:

Including everyone is a very difficult thing. I think there should be places for hypersensitive people with fewer bright lights and noises, but also places for people who need to move and make noises that could bother others, like vocal stims. For me, talking on the telephone or ordering something in person is a challenge, and I much prefer online options.

Celebrating and nurturing Autistic preferences for connection means accepting that non-traditional and remote forms of interaction can be equally valuable.

Connecting sustainably, No. 6: Embrace diversity—and diverse relationship models

Why is this needed?

Because they don't always automatically "get" NT social norms, most Autistic people by necessity evolve as best they can into scientists of human interaction. In the process, many develop their own modes of interaction and visions for relationships that do not conform to traditional models. From Abramowski's (she/her) perspective, "I think the expectation for people to be cookie-cutter copies of each other doesn't allow neuro-divergent people to flourish."

Creating new systems

As Autistic thought leader Vishen Lakhiani notes in his book, *The Code of the Extraordinary Mind* (2019), Autistic people's brains see things differently, giving them insights into the "codes" by which NT society operates. Thus, they are often life-hackers. They tend to develop their own systems for functioning and succeeding—and may decide an unconventional approach works best for them.

This journey can sometimes be bumpy. Some of our respondents wished they had had more guidance around relationships or reported wishing they had learned about the "concept of sexuality" in a more "explicit" way (Raj, he/him). Others, such as Balfour (she/her), who in her freshman year of college, "got really quickly involved in an emotionally/psychologically abusive relationship," found themselves in untenable situations.

Relationships between Autistic people may be more likely to reflect a good fit in intensity and contact needs. Baik (she/her) explains:

> I am myself from the get go, and that makes [people] either love or hate me. I am also very intense in all relationships (like I want to speak to my friends every day, pretty much) and a LOT of non-Autistics aren't like that.

Some "mixed" friendships can work, as one respondent (she/her) found: "I tried befriending non-Autistic people, but it can be a challenge as I can appear over-friendly or attach to them quickly without knowing their perspective of me. But, some stayed with me, though."

Each relationship poses unique challenges for Autistic people, from navigating the initial phase to aligning interaction and communication modes. Being open to negotiating these elements characterizes true inclusivity and respect. One respondent (she/they) offers some insights into the process:

> Starting a friendship is the most difficult part for me, as I typically don't want to bother others and don't mind being alone too much... I am a pretty loyal friend, although I may come across as clingy at times. I find it difficult to keep in touch via text and telephone, because finding the right words takes a lot of energy.

Embracing the weird

Step 1 discussed the importance of families embracing the quirkiness of the Autistic people in their homes, which in turn helps Autistic people also accept their differences. It can take a while to accept and honor their own unique qualities, but, at some point in their life journey, many Autistic people decide to embrace the weird. They may have found accepting communities and relationships, or they may have decided to look for them, rather than settling for being tolerated. Bridge (they/them) explains that while they struggled earlier in life, they now "take pride" in their "weirdness" because they know people who accept their "weirdness and 'eccentricity.'" Harrington (she/her) says, "I embrace being weird and different," and Nora (she/her) affirms, "I don't care if people think I'm a bit weird."

Connecting sustainably, No. 7: Understand differences in body language, social cues, and processing speeds

Why is this needed?

Being aware that Autistic people often experience and process information, emotions, and sensory input differently (more slowly, more intensely, or otherwise), can also help us make respectful choices. Whether initiating a friendship or developing a romantic or other relationship, taking the time to check in and be sensitive about interaction is a crucial element of any relationship. Nied (she/they) explains this very clearly:

> Something I've always struggled with is naming and verbalizing feelings, so I often have delayed reactions when it comes to intimacy and sex. If my partner were to ask me if I was okay, or something was working/not working, I often don't know in the moment... I think what I'd appreciate the most is if people would slow down in their explanations of certain concepts, especially ones involving multiple

parts. I do have the capacity to understand, I just need you to meet me halfway. Also, something I've found helpful with previous partners is that if I'm not able to verbalize if something intimate feels good or not, I use my hands a lot, so I can wiggle my fingers if something is good, or I can sort of tap my fingers if I need to stop, and so on.

Practicing patience

Since relationships are, in Ierubino's (he/him) words, "important for everyone," he wishes people would be more patient: "[I] often have difficulty communicating and choosing the right words to say." Using assistive technologies and allowing plenty of time are just two elements that can improve communication for some, but other challenges may arise. Vu (he/him) describes a range of hurdles he encounters when trying to connect with people:

> I struggle to figure out how to process conversations or respond to them, especially if people dive into topics or experiences I'm not familiar with. While I try to be interested in other people, it's hard when I have a hard time coming up with questions to ask or anything relevant to say to them.

For one respondent (NP), "It's really hard. I don't know how to talk to people, so I have to wait for people to talk to me and hope they ask things I can answer so we can talk."

One thing many Autistic people find helpful given these varied communication styles is scripting or planning conversational tactics in advance. Marsh (they/them) explains that when they are meeting up with someone:

> I plan out the conversation ahead of time. Sometimes it can go so far as a script more akin to what I might use for a podcast. It works okay, but I always need an escape route and I have to respect my very limited capacity.

Deciphering signals and tone

Interpreting NT signals is a big challenge for many respondents, including Vu (he/him):

> The hardest part of friendships with neurotypicals is being able to read body language and social cues. I have a hard time knowing how to joke around people or how to see if someone is sarcastic or not as I can take things out of context easily.

For others, such as Tino (he/him), sensory and physical differences can create barriers to friendship: "Neurotypicals need to understand my body issues. If I leave the room, it does not mean I don't want to be with you. If I look away, I am trying to listen."

Challenges with tone also loom large for many, as in Chloe's (she/her) view that people "misinterpret me or assume my tone wrongly," or Cordeiro's (they/them) experience of being misunderstood: "I don't get when they're annoyed or upset and [so] people consider me to be inconsiderate... I simply ask questions and they consider me to be rude." Adding to these factors, many Autistic youth report either being prone to dropping the ball on connections because of overwhelm or, conversely, tending to overwhelm potential friends by talking or reaching out "too much."

But awareness around these differences—from sensory and movement needs, to difficulties reading NT body language and social cues, to cultivating a balanced level of interaction—can facilitate genuine neurodiverse relationships of all sorts. Such sustainable connections integrate and honor the physiological/neurological needs and communication styles of both/all parties, enabling people to interact and express themselves in a variety of ways, whether that involves more time, increased mutual clarity around tone/signals/intention, the use of assistive technology, or any other useful adaptation.

Connecting sustainably, No. 8: Understand that masking is exhausting

Why is this needed?

In short, masking is pretending you are neurotypical. Whether consciously or unconsciously, willingly or unwillingly, with "coaching" or without, convincingly or not, many Autistic people learn to mask in order to better fit into the dominant NT culture. As Walzer (NP) explains:

> I had to mimic and mime my way from preteen into teen and then young adulthood. I was wired differently and had to act a part that was not always me. I learned to cope, adapt, adjust, shape-shift, and be chameleon-like to exist in a neurotypical world.

But masking takes an enormous emotional, psychological, and physical toll on us. This can be particularly true for intersectional Autistic youth belonging to other marginalized groups who may also mask for similar reasons, such as Black people feeling forced to "act white," or LGBTQIA+ people experiencing pressure to "seem straight." In Chloe's (she/her) words, "It's a communication minefield, and it takes up so much energy, leaving me exhausted." Cordeiro (they/them) notes they just "can't keep up this front," even though "I worry sometimes that people are making decisions about me, about whether to include me, to be friends with me, or to even consider me worth their time, based on how I present myself." For Truty (she/her), the toll of masking during adolescence was devastating:

> Of course, now we know that I was masking to fit in, and I had been pretty good at blending in before puberty—then things like flirting and cliques and pop culture all hit at once. Without knowing it, I was working so hard to keep up. I really didn't know that I was struggling, so I didn't know to ask for help. By 14, I hit a wall, and it got ugly.

A suicide attempt made me reset my entire self. I had to rebuild, which I'm really proud of myself for being able to do, but I shouldn't have had to.

One respondent (she/her) explains how her mask "slips off" the more she gets to know someone, "My voice starts to sound more monotone, less expressive. My facial expressions begin to look more blank or relaxed. The amount of eye contact that I give others begins to decrease." By calling attention to how people tend to correct harmless social quirks, and by working against pressures to mask, we can "erode away at neurotypical culture" (Marsh, they/them).

Building better spaces and cultures

Creating safe, inclusive, respectful spaces and cultures enables Autistic people to "drop the mask" and use their energy for healthier things, like friendship, as Gallant (she/her) suggests:

> I struggle with the expectations to be around people and always be masking and friendly. This got worse as I transitioned into adulthood. For example, my first year in a college dorm I had no place to be alone, drop my mask, and stim...safe spaces for autistic people would greatly improve my situation.

Such spaces and interactions reduce or eliminate pressure to mask, and allow Autistic people to be loved, seen, and accepted for who they are.

When we can be open about our identity and neurology, we feel liberated. For example, Jenny noticed that after "coming out" as Autistic, she experienced a much lower stress level in both public speaking and personal interactions. One respondent (she/they) has noticed they are masking less post-diagnosis: "I have been getting more confident about myself and less worried that people will think I am different, because I now know that I actually am different, but that that isn't a bad thing."

Paying the price

Sometimes masking can feel "necessary," even when it comes at a high cost. One respondent (she/her) frequently makes this choice, "I do not do it to fit in, I do it so that my life is easier. People respond to you better when you behave a certain way." One respondent (she/her) has masked for more serious reasons, "Pretending to be as normal as possible—masking—was essential to survival in my house. It helped to minimize the emotional abuse. I learned that being 'different' was wrong and shameful." And some of our respondents, such as "pro-masker" Baik (she/her) and Emily (she/her), feel neutral to positive about masking under certain circumstances. Emily says, "I hope I blend in rather than strangers thinking I am different—I never aim to stick out/get attention. I think I can mask enough to pass through a scenario with a stranger."

Some Autistics are more proficient in masking than others, but that doesn't mean they want to have to mask to succeed in connecting with others. Many AFAB (assigned female at birth) Autistic people encounter this issue, including Chloe (she/her), who worries "especially about Autistic girls, because some of us mask autism so well...people assume we understand and we aren't struggling." One respondent (she/her) shares that:

> When I am out in the world, I am an actress playing a part, and I play it very well. I've created a character that most people find endearing, lovable. Most people who do not know me do not know that this person does not exist.

For many, as for Maclean (NP), the personal price paid for masking is very high, "Most days I mask myself to function [as 'normal'], yet that gets tiring to the point of where I am not being able to do anything, as I just automatically shut down."

Being aware of the many facets of masking, and ensuring that it's never required for you or those around you, can help Autistic people and those who care about them connect in deep and lasting ways. As Kimble (she/her) says, she feels truly accepted "when other people want to be around me and like me for who I am and not what I pretend to be sometimes (masking)."

Conclusion: Fostering healthy, positive relationships

Making and growing connections can be a little more complicated for Autistic people, but our respondents highlight many ways to encourage worthwhile, mutually beneficial interactions. This may mean leaning toward inter-Autistic friendships, as for Forrester (any/varies), who says, "I make friends fairly easily, but it turns out most of my friends are on the spectrum. For those who are on the spectrum, we relate to each other well from the get-go." Or it may simply entail fostering spaces and cultures that enable people to find positive relationships over time, like Kimble (she/her), who has found that "there are some people who do understand or are more understanding than others and these are the people I try to stay around."

SUMMARY GUIDANCE:
#ActuallyAutistic practical tips for connection through friendships and other relationships

- Understand that many different types of relationships can be fulfilling, not just those favored in neurotypical cultures.
- Realize that Autistic people often connect well together.
- Allow ample time for processing and communication.
- Remember that respectful language and actions are prerequisites for healthy relationships.
- Use common interests as a basis for connection.

- Remember that environments that don't encourage masking are more likely to nurture healthy connections.

REFLECTION QUESTIONS

? What would help you "find your person/people"?

? What is your perspective on the "double empathy problem"?

? Is there anything you could do to make the spaces you inhabit feel safer for, and more encouraging of, neurodiverse social connections?

? Have you ever masked or pressured someone else to mask?

? What sorts of relationships matter to you? What types of interactions do you prefer in those relationships?

Step 3

Encourage Welcoming Activities and Social Events

Real inclusion means you are looking to identify and utilize the talents that I can bring to any activity. It doesn't mean you are looking for ways to drag my body into the action and plans that everyone else already has in motion.

—ANONYMOUS (HE/HIM)

"To feel accepted and included is a happy feeling," says Ierubino (he/him). Many contributors expressed the sentiment of wanting to be included. After all, spending time with their peers and exploring various activities are two of the main ways tweens, teens, and young adults figure out who they are and what interests them in life. As Autistic young people transition to independence and adulthood at their own pace, connections and experience gained in the social arena can bolster their growth, opportunities, confidence, and success. But inclusion efforts must be considerate and intentional if they are to truly affirm and uplift all of us in both our differences and similarities.

There are lots of different ways to include people, and not all people feel included in the same ways and in the same spaces.

Some activities that have a purpose of being inclusive can actually have the opposite effect. Corrado (she/her) explains that ice-breaker games are one example of this, especially if they take place in a sensory-overwhelming environment with large groups of people. She says, "I find ice-breaker games like 'what is the most embarrassing thing that happened to you' exclusive."

Thus, rather than taking a generic "checklist" approach to inclusion, we suggest carefully considering the unique needs of all potential participants, especially marginalized people. This chapter asks us to consider ways we can self-advocate and accommodate those around us to encourage and facilitate the most inclusive activities and events.

Encouraging welcoming activities and social events, No. 1: Invite people to places they are comfortable with

Why is this needed?

An invitation to participate in an activity, however small or large scale, is a small step toward inclusion and willingness to learn, engage, and enjoy time with another person. Going further, though, people must consider the environments they are inviting people into, including both the physical surroundings and the behaviors/acceptance of those who might be in that space. Specifically, we can consider the sensory stimuli in the space we are inviting someone into, and whether or not someone's sensory profile is a good match, as well as whether that environment could be updated. We can also facilitate outings with both NT and ND people. And we can support events hosted by marginalized communities, when possible.

Considering sensory sensitivities

Public spaces (or anywhere outside one's personal residence) often contain hard-to-control sensory stimuli. When inviting someone to a new space, consider that person's sensory sensitivities and how they might be managed in the new environment. For Corrado (she/her), this means a smaller group size, "I need a setting that is not sensory-overwhelming, or a large in-person group where people talk over each other." Cordeiro (they/them) says they sometimes get invited to places, but people don't change their plans to accommodate them. Cordeiro explains, "They don't understand that I have different needs. They continue with loud noises and fast-paced activities without considering that I might prefer things to be kind of slower and quieter."

Henderson (she/her) says the smallest actions can go a long way in making an invitation more welcoming/inclusive. For example:

> Things like asking if the music volume is too loud... I always worry about being left out of group activities because I am not good in loud or crowded situations, so when my friend was asking in advance about accommodations she could make so that I could come to an event she was holding, it made me extremely happy. When I thanked her for being so understanding and inviting me even though it might be a little more complicated, she replied with, "I wouldn't dream of leaving you out." That one sentence made my heart feel very full (metaphorically speaking)! Being autistic means that you hear all the time about how annoying your condition is and what an inconvenience you are if you take steps to try and help yourself, so being explicitly told that I am wanted and welcome and not a bother is really important to me.

In an article interview titled "'No You're Not'—A Portrait Of Autistic Women," (Barnes, 2022), Heidi explains that while working as a musician, there is an expectation to be sociable, and people assume that Heidi is comfortable being sociable. But Heidi's comfort is a direct effect of a controlled environment. Heidi says:

I'm only confident because we've [Heidi and partner Belinda] created an environment that we're in complete control of... We've built this show, we've got distance from the audience, we've even created a sensory experience that we like and we do our own sound. So things are not necessarily as they seem. (Barnes, 2022, para. 18–19)

Being thoughtful and proactive about potential sensory sensitivities—whether your own or others'—can be an essential part of healthy, enjoyable social interaction and other activities.

Encouraging activities with a diverse group of people

There are a lot of different factors that add up to a pleasant social gathering, and while these factors will vary from person to person, some survey contributors mentioned that it's sometimes more comfortable for Autistic people if other neurodivergent people are also present. Chloe (she/her) says that she feels most included when people understand her fully, adding, "This tends to only be something that is common in Autistic spaces with Autistic and neurodivergent people though." Corrado (she/her) also says it helps to know that "there is at least one other neurodivergent person in the group" or to be with people who "at least are familiar with autism."

Supporting events run for and by marginalized communities

Other respondents said that they are more comfortable entering spaces and events that are hosted by Autistic people or other marginalized communities. Ierubino (he/him) shares this perspective:

I went to a convention for one of my special interests. It really felt like the most inclusive event I have ever been to. This makes me think that if more people went to events run by and for marginalized communities, they would see examples of how inclusive communities work. The more you engage with others different than you, the more you can learn and feel comfortable with all types of people.

In another example, s.e. smith details the restful yet exhilarating experience of being in an inclusive space in an article for the *Disability Visibility* anthology, edited by Alice Wong, titled "The Beauty of Spaces Created for and by Disabled People." smith recounts attending a dance performance choreographed by Alice Sheppard in collaboration with Laurel Lawson, and writes, "It is very rare, as a disabled person, that I have an intense sense of belonging, of being not just tolerated in a space but actively owning it" (Wong, 2020, p.272). smith describes some of the aspects of those surroundings that signal inclusivity: the presence of wheelchair and scooter users, an American Sign Language interpreter, canes, prosthetic limbs, and a stage model and audio transcriptions for a blind attendee. smith says, "The first *social* setting where you come to the giddy understanding that this is a place for disabled people is a momentous one, and one worth lingering over" (Wong, 2020, p.272); and describes these spaces of communal belonging as having "a deep *rightness* that comes from not having to explain or justify your existence."

Encouraging welcoming activities and social events, No. 2: Make accommodations without too much overt attention to disability

Why is this needed?
Inclusive activities not only have spaces and roles for everyone, but they allow everyone to participate in the ways they wish to. Additionally, they don't draw too much attention to any disability or modifications, rather, accommodations are a natural, built-in part of the event or activity. This often

requires planning—either on the part of the self-advocate to predict and communicate needs and preferences, or on the part of a caring relative, teacher, or friend to initiate dialogue to better understand how to design or approach truly inclusive activities.

School individualized education plans (IEPs) can sometimes be a way to formally communicate accommodations in the educational setting, but life is so nuanced that it's impossible to predict every situation that will arise. Despite the challenge, this work is necessary. In an interview for Wellcome Collection, Lauren draws attention to the difficulties she sometimes endures to prepare for an outing: "It could take me five hours to leave my house, which could include me being sick and having multiple panic attacks" (Barnes, 2022, para. 10). Harrington (she/her; survey contributor) expresses the frustration of others acting as if accommodations are a burden: "Too many people act like accommodating us is a burden on *them*."

Both NT and Autistic people being open to regular communication about inclusion is key. Furthermore, NTs must realize that self-advocacy can be exhausting, so the more often they (NT people) can be vigilant of when and how they can best welcome/accommodate for the ND people they care about, the better off everyone will be.

Avoiding token inclusion

One Autistic teenage respondent (he/him) also diagnosed with cerebral palsy shared his frustration with the token inclusion he experiences in his school. He describes how he felt when his gym teacher gave him a modified activity (keeping score) because the teacher was worried that people would bump into him and he would fall on the ground. "I'm big with math, but I'd prefer actually playing a game. I didn't come to gym class to sit on the sidelines, did I? ... This made me feel like a baby, and it was embarrassing. This isn't real inclusion."

This also happens with this teen's peers:

If I'm playing in a basketball game in gym or at a park, people only rarely pass the ball to me, or they might pass the ball to me and then immediately ask for it back. It's as if letting me touch the ball is enough to make me feel included. This isn't real inclusion. I don't feel like part of a team if I am only allowed to touch a ball and pass it back to someone right away. I want to be a player. I want to make a difference. I want to compete.

Ableism or other misconceptions about disability will cause exclusion, even when people think they are being nice or accommodating.

Similarly, forcing people to participate or join activities they are uncomfortable with isn't real inclusion. In the same Wellcome Collection interview mentioned earlier in this chapter, another interviewee, Elinor, recalls how difficult recess was as a young child, watching the other children from the sidelines while teachers encouraged her to join them:

I was just praying for rain so we could go inside where there was structure. I could draw or read a book and be in the corner where it was just easier. But the teachers would come up behind me and push me forward saying, "Go play, Elinor, go play." I'd just literally be frozen. It felt like a dream of being in a snow globe where everything is falling. I also had a very vivid sense that I had come from somewhere else and I wanted to go back there. I would look up at the sky and think, "I've had enough of this now, can I go back please?" (Barnes, 2022, para. 27)

Acknowledging but not drawing too much attention to disability

The teen (he/him) discussing gym class above says that he doesn't like the fact that his physical disability is the first thing that people notice about him. "Whenever my eyes and the eyes of a stranger meet, they usually stare at my legs for a few seconds when they can. (I have orthotics on both legs.)" But if the attention doesn't linger or lead to stereotyping and isolation, and instead to understanding and acceptance, this can foster inclusion. Some contributors said that it's helpful when people try to understand and notice (not ignore) difference and disability, being aware and accommodating, and asking people what they need. Cordeiro (they/them) says, "When somebody goes out of their way to understand, I feel accepted and included."

Encouraging welcoming activities and social events, No. 3: Treat people as competent, interesting, and appreciated

Why is this needed?
Knowing that other people enjoy being around you is essential to feeling welcomed and included. We can be sensitive to the types of social interactions we invite people into, considering how we (NT or ND) can foster real inclusion. And we can expect those around us to treat us and others well in social contexts. As one contributor (he/him) says, "It's not enough to tolerate the presence of someone standing near you while you are talking. That's not inclusion. You need to engage them in the conversation you are having, show interest, and ask questions."

Presuming competence and avoiding stereotypes
A basic tenet to being inclusive is presuming competence. As Tino (he/him) explains, "I feel accepted when people talk directly to me and talk to me as if I understand, which I do! I like it when others include me in the conversation, even if I don't respond." One respondent (NP) asks people to not get annoyed with them: "Just give me time and don't help unless I want it." Josey (he/him) explains that sometimes NT people can overstep in conversations by assuming they understand Autistic people:

One example of people trying to be inclusive but ending up not really being that helpful is when they may say or do things to include themselves in conversation or think they know what you feel, but they really don't know how you feel.

Stereotypes about autism can also complicate social interactions and be obstacles to inclusion. Liu (she/her) says:

I find it frustrating when people make assumptions about autistic people, even when they mean well. For example, "You must be great with computers!" Or when they patronize us or make assumptions about our abilities. People sometimes see us as stupid, incompetent, childlike, and so on, when we struggle, or appear autistic. Or they see us passing as neurotypical and assume we don't have additional struggles. I also find it hard to hear how autism is still seen as a lesser way of being and something shameful to be removed or separated from the person.

In conversations about neurodiversity, Liu adds, NTs should listen to what Autistic people have to say about autism and amplify their messages rather than talking over them. This starts with trust and confidence in Autistic voices and expertise.

Listening with respect and humility

Many respondents said they appreciate genuine connections with people who are understanding about different communication styles and needs. One respondent (she/her) says Autistic people rarely get invited to parties and are often isolated from mainstream society, and suggests, "People should understand them more or get to know a bit about them as well as being patient." Baik (she/her) says she feels included "when people around me are genuine and aren't putting on a front (I hate 'politeness' and all that), and they treat me as an equal."

Some contributors feel the most included when they can spend time one-on-one with someone who is patient, in a quiet space where they can really focus on the conversation. Marsh (they/them) says:

> I am at my best socially in one-on-one quiet social settings, where both I and the other person are almost completely focused on the conversation and hearing and reflecting the other person. This is very hard to pull off, so happens rarely, and generally with older adults aged 40+.

One respondent (she/her) says she feels most included in conversations with her girlfriend, who really listens to her and "validates" her. In general, conversations with people who are patient and follow the lead of others they are conversing with are more inclusive. Maclean (NP) says life is very unfair for Autistic people, so it helps for others to "be able to be patient, and if we feel ready, let them speak up for us, yet ask us first." Maclean adds that it's good to "find a safe place for us to share our stories."

Encouraging welcoming activities and social events, No. 4: Express concern for others and allow people to speak freely about their interests

Why is this needed?

As with Step 2 above, enjoyment of other people's company naturally depends on the opportunity to share mutually appealing activities and discussion topics. This doesn't mean the topic and level of enthusiasm must be equally matched by both parties, but some connection (and active demonstration of that connection) should exist. Showing interest in conversations is a natural extension of caring for another person, and, as many contributors point out, demonstrating this concern for the well-being and interests of others is so important to making them feel included and accepted.

Paying attention and showing interest in conversations

Paying attention to the interests of others helps them feel included. This is especially true for Autistic people, who often feel unseen and unheard. Several respondents shared how they appreciated time with people who included them in discussions and accepted their interests and chosen topics. Bridge (they/them) says they feel accepted when people "understand and accept the things I talk about as normal and good or even funny...those who look at me and see the beauty and monstrosity of who I am and like what they see." Maclean (NP) says it helps when people are "talking to me like a proper person and really showing interest in what I have to say and what I can do." One respondent (she/they) says, "I like it when people are interested in interacting with me, especially when they are interested in and want to hear about my special interests. I appreciate the effort of people asking how they can make me feel more comfortable."

Vu (he/him) describes just how powerful paying attention to special interests can be:

I remember sitting in a tutoring center at a community college when I decided to share an opinion I had about Valentine's Day. I decided to go on and on about my thoughts on Valentine's Day and assumed that no one would care to listen to me. However, my friend at the time (who sat next to me) decided to put away her laptop, fold her hands, and pay attention to me, listening with intent and open ears. It was a euphoric feeling as I rarely had encounters where people highly valued my opinions or thoughts so it caught me off-guard at first, but in the end, I became more willing and grateful enough to continue talking about my beliefs and viewpoints. I'm most comfortable and happy when I get to keep talking about the things I care about without being interrupted, and having people around me that value my perspective and would love to hear more about what I have to say.

Feeling truly heard is a powerful and necessary experience for all of us. But it can be all too rare for Autistic young people, who often feel sidelined or ignored, and thus spend lots of time listening or tuning out. Being able to express ourselves and feel that someone cares and is interested in what we have to say is an integral part of welcoming environments and interactions.

Expressing concern for others' well-being

Mental health is a big concern for many tweens, teens, and young adults. Autistic young people often face challenges to their well-being related to the difficulties that inherently arise when growing up Autistic in a neurotypical world. Bidon (she/her) shares how she appreciates when people are genuinely concerned about her mental health and ask her what they can do if she appears to need help:

I remember my sophomore roommate was worried when I was hospitalized the second time. Another friend was worried the fourth time I was hospitalized and let me go hiking [with them]. Another friend I made was genuinely worried and didn't make fun of me for being clumsy. Wow!

When we (NT or ND) make time to demonstrate our concern and care for those around us, we foster real inclusion, validate self-worth, and grow real friendships.

Encouraging welcoming activities and social events, No. 5: Be open to varied communication methods

Why is this needed?

Communication barriers due to varied communication methods and preferences should be considered as differences to actively accommodate and not the fault of any one particular person. If Autistic people learn about their particular communication preferences and needs and share those with their homes and/or communities, an inclusive infrastructure can begin to be built around them. Learning about communication differences and sharing that knowledge can help others be more sensitive and accommodating to potential needs. Being open to learning and growing is an essential mindset to get started.

Encouraging greater awareness/knowledge of communication differences

Doing your own research on advice given by Autistic experts is always a great start to learning about communication differences. Moody (she/her) says increased knowledge in this area is needed:

> I find it extremely difficult to make friends and communicate with those I don't know, but I think guidance digitally, in books, and surrounding me would help, like if more people were more aware that there are people who have difficulty communicating with others...because the world we live in is very much speech and language driven, when, in reality, many people just find it easier to communicate in other ways.

Being open

Even if there is a lack of awareness around specific communication differences or modes of communicating (including assistive technologies), being patient and open to learning will help in any new situation. Maclean (NP) says it helps if people accept a slower or otherwise varied communication pace and don't try to "yell" or "growl" when people take the time they need to express themselves; "Also, don't ever try to speak for me, as in trying to form any sentences, and if I lose what I am saying, just remind me where I was up to." One respondent (NP) also asks for patience and understanding of different communication styles, "I wish people would know that when I can't say a lot, it doesn't mean I don't want to talk. I want to talk, and if I'm slow, leave it alone."

Another respondent (he/him) agrees that "learning to communicate clearly with us and being patient goes a long way" and acknowledges that it can be challenging to engage with someone who prefers, or is accustomed to, a different communication style. He explains:

> Often, allistic people think I'm being rude or sarcastic because they assume there is subtext or sarcasm in what I say, so even a compliment comes across as an insult, and I wish people would believe me when I tell them I meant exactly what I said and nothing else. It also would be nice if, when I ask for clarification on what someone means or if they mean what they said, they don't seem aggravated at having to explain it to me.

Communication is arguably the most vital aspect of social interaction, and as such we need to pay attention to how we facilitate it for ourselves and others. Becoming familiar with, and accepting of, varied communication styles, technologies, and needs is one fundamental way to promote mutually respectful, enjoyable interaction. Being open and patient when differences or difficulties arise is another key tool for improvement in this crucial area.

Conclusion: Coming together in welcoming ways

Genuinely inclusive gatherings entail taking several important factors into account. When we honor these five facets of welcoming social gatherings, we make it possible for young people of all neurologies and abilities to join their peers (and others) in uplifting, healing, constructive, even transformative ways.

SUMMARY GUIDANCE:
#ActuallyAutistic practical tips for activities and social events

- Get to know your own preferences and needs around participating in social and recreational activities.
- Be open to different ways of communicating and making friends.
- Get to know someone before inviting them into a new space, or ask them about their interests, preferred environments, and so on when/after inviting them somewhere.
- If you are Autistic, consider ways you are comfortable self-advocating for the environments you prefer.
- Understand that accommodations might be necessary prior to and during an activity or event.
- Be patient in conversations, and look for ways to connect over mutual interests.
- Continue the conversation on inclusion. Get (and give) feedback on inclusion efforts, from leadership and education to physical spaces and available resources and technologies.

REFLECTION QUESTIONS

? What are your communication style preferences? What do you find challenging? What efforts can be made to bridge the gap between different preferences?

? [If Autistic] How do you self-advocate for your socialization preferences? Where can you improve in this area?

? [If neurotypical] What proactive, inclusive things are you doing to invite the Autistic people around you to activities or events with you? Where can you improve in this area?

? How do you know if the events you are setting up or participating in are truly inclusive? How can you ensure this for the future?

Step 4

Nurture Autism-Friendly Practices in School

Just having the right people with the right attitude and mind-set, along with having patience, was always important to me.

—MACLEAN (NP)

Why do we need welcoming schools?

Our middle and high school years leave a profound and permanent imprint on most of us. Transitions between elementary and middle school, from middle to high school, and out of high school also carry a great deal of weight for Autistic youth. Our contributors had plenty to say about this part of their lives!

In schools, Autistic tweens and teens endure and/or benefit from extensive interactions with their ND and NT peers, along with teachers and staff, school cultures, curricula, policies, and built environments. These various elements of the learning experience can have a powerful negative or positive impact on growth and self-esteem, along with academic learning, making schools perhaps the key formative facet of growing up. Similarly, alternative learning settings, such as vocational schools or homeschooling, shape youth in profound ways. Generating evolution in these vital spaces can make a huge difference for Autistic youth as they set off on their unique journeys into adulthood.

We need to build autism-friendly environments, learning materials, and cultures in every educational setting so that Autistic people can emerge from their teen years with not only the necessary knowledge, practical tools, and skills, but also the inner strengths that are absolutely essential to navigating their next steps. Integrating wisdom from those who have lived experience with these contexts will ensure that the changes we work for actually benefit Autistic youth. As with every other section, we hope this information will be useful for Autistic students, as well as for anyone who wants to make schools a better place for them, including teachers and families.

Finding approaches that truly serve students

The "right attitude and mindset" and "patience" Maclean (NP) mentions above shouldn't be such a big ask in schools, especially those that serve diverse populations. Yet our respondents reported significant challenges and suffering in their school years. Moody's (she/her) experience is fairly representative:

> I remember a lot from school, from getting bullied to not being chosen every single time when we played basketball in the PE/sport class. But one thing I wish was different was how teachers taught their lessons. Rather than teaching toxic systems like "you have to work hard," they could have adapted learning styles to different people and different needs.

Harrington (she/her) faced teachers who lacked both empathy and basic awareness: "Accepting teachers were rare. Most teachers either didn't know how to adapt to my disabilities or forgot about them, leaving me to flounder. One memorable contingent outright antagonized me and refused to honor my ADA [Americans with Disabilities Act]-given rights."

Many students also find themselves struggling as less support becomes available over the years, adding to the stress of these transitions. Cordeiro (they/them) describes such a scenario:

My experience hasn't been great. I struggled to read and write a lot as a child, but was still very smart. I was in "special ed" in elementary school, but lost all of my supports as soon as I got to middle school because I could get As by myself. No one realized that I was struggling, and I spent most of my time overcompensating. Basically, by the time I got to high school, school was my entire life. No one realized that there was a problem because I was a straight-A student.

Autistic students and those who care about them know we need to do better throughout the educational system, from the interpersonal to the institutional levels. That evolution starts with welcoming school cultures.

Nurturing all neurologies—and all people

Schools that welcome and celebrate differences offer students enormous advantages in personal growth, confidence, and self-esteem. McHugh (he/him) describes one such place:

The school...worked to ensure that everyone connected to the school community—pupils, staff, and parents—understood the importance of basic values, including kindness and respect for others, no matter what differences there were. Looking back, this helped me to feel a great sense of inclusion.

However, most schools have room for growth. The input of the particular Autistic students in a given classroom or school is also key, so if you are a parent or educator, this is a great time to listen. And students, we hope this section (along with the rest of the book) will encourage you to find your voice, whether vocalized, written, or otherwise expressed!

The following concrete, clear practices foster acceptance and awareness in school communities, enabling Autistic tweens and teens to feel comfortable, included, and focused—so that they can learn as both students and human beings. We've also included tips for alternative teen learning contexts.

MIDDLE AND HIGH SCHOOL

Nurturing welcoming schools, No. 1: Pursue earlier diagnosis/ self-awareness, if possible

Many of us wish all environments were fundamentally accepting of all differences. In the real world, however, a lot needs to change to even begin approaching this ideal—especially in schools. Knowledge of one's own neurology, and of autism in general, can help Autistic students gain self-awareness and confidence, which can mitigate some of the less ideal experiences they may encounter during their school years. And that knowledge can also help them—and their teachers—find tools and strategies to improve both social interactions and academic achievement. Many struggle terribly without this information.

Cohen (she/her), who was not diagnosed until later in life, says:

> I was constantly misunderstood and teachers did not like me because (among other reasons) I asked too many questions, and expected them to mean what they said. I think

having understood what autism is and that I am autistic would have helped a great deal.

Similarly, Stringfield (he/him) notes, "I often struggled with socializing and social anxiety in high school, and I believe if I had knowledge of my diagnosis and methods to deal with the issues I was having, things would have been much better." In addition to fostering mental health, clarity around neurodivergence can help enormously with academics. This was certainly true for Cordeiro (they/them), who, after being diagnosed as a teen, "was finally given supports, which included access to spoken information (in lieu of written) and extra time on tests."

According to our respondents, the earlier an Autistic young person learns about themselves the better, because a lack of awareness can not only impact school learning, but have lifelong repercussions. For Balfour (she/her):

> High school was really hard—I was really depressed and anxious, doing a lot of self-harm. It's hard to say what would have made things better other than a diagnosis! If I had known about my autism and ADHD, I would have been able to learn how to live healthier in my brain as a child and wouldn't have developed a lot of the unhealthy coping mechanisms that make my life harder now.

A lack of awareness can impede learning, cause many types of trauma, and have lifelong personal, familial, and societal repercussions. That's why so many Autistic young people suggest figuring out (through formal or informal diagnostic channels), and being open about, autism as early as possible. It's empowering to know who you are, and to be able to use that knowledge to figure out what you need to succeed. The rest of this chapter focuses on important facets of what that might entail.

Nurturing welcoming schools, No. 2:
Separate learning settings
from social settings

While meaningful personal interaction can certainly occur in educational environments, many Autistic students dislike and/or do not benefit from the constant combination of socializing and learning found in many middle and high schools. Some resent the imposition of "social skills" curricula into their school day. For a variety of reasons, some have a hard time with the increasingly common "group work" model of learning. Others find the constant social whirl of the typical classroom sensorially or personally debilitating—or, like Jenny, cannot focus on academics and interaction at the same time.

Fox (she/her) found that the social aspects of the classroom increasingly presented a barrier to learning:

> As the social side of school increased with age, my ability to pay attention in the classrooms decreased. I was unable to socially keep up with my peers without completely draining myself—this meant that when it came to learning, I was exhausted and found it harder and harder to concentrate in the classrooms due to sensory overload.

Distinguishing between social and educational contexts can make space for more effective, deeper learning. Looking back on their school years, Marsh (they/them) suggests that encouraging focus in Autistic learners entails two key elements: developing classrooms and other environments that facilitate each individual's ability to focus, and nurturing every student's passions to enhance their learning (more on this below). In their view, "the key to Autistic learning would have to be some sort of independent learning setting free from the social element and chock-full of material that suits the individual's interest spikes."

Where possible, it can be helpful for Autistic students

when schools keep the classroom focus on learning, or at least provide opportunities and environments in which they can shift from expending their energy on deploying social skills to studying the subject matter at hand.

Nurturing welcoming schools, No. 3: Emphasize supportive and respectful attitudes and behaviors for teachers and staff

Schools are for learning, right? But many are set up and run in such a way that Autistic students can't benefit from that fundamental promise. Caring, informed educators and other school employees can ensure that students of all neurologies and abilities are able to fulfill their potential. As Ierubino (he/him) explains, "Once I had some teachers who understood me, I was able to learn how to be a better student—one who could learn."

What does this comprehension entail? Several respondents suggested that if teachers had a better understanding of autism, things would improve. Promoting understanding could involve sharing informative materials, including autism-awareness/acceptance workshops (run by Autistic professionals for teachers and staff as part of required professional development), starting affinity groups, and more. Autistic students and their families can advocate for greater awareness in these ways, but they are also things that administrators and educators themselves can work for—for their own benefit as well as that of their students.

For some students, one understanding adult can make all the difference, as with one respondent's (she/her) "compassionate" drama teacher/faculty head. She says the teacher "reinforced to me that if you give people a 'heads up,' it can help you when you need it most."

In addition to support, awareness, and acceptance, Autistic

students need teachers who are educated enough to treat their students as unique individuals worthy and deserving of respect. This includes seeing each person for themselves, rather than labeling and then grouping accordingly:

> Looking back, I feel like I was definitely placed in a box as a student. I was one of three students in my graduating class with an Autism diagnosis, so we were placed in almost all the same classes... I was a mediocre student at best, and I had few teachers who I really connected with... I constantly had to remind myself that grades do not measure intelligence. (Macedo, he/him)

Schools, teachers, and staff that respectfully involve students in shaping key aspects of their own education both enable and foster engagement. Chen (she/her) appreciated being a part of the team drafting her IEP: "It made me feel like a respected individual with autonomy in determining my own path—an uncommon experience for autistic people in many sectors of society." In order to take a truly inclusive and student-affirming approach, educators themselves must be educated about intersectionality, neurodiversity, and more. And both educators and administrators must be willing to experiment with new forms of interaction and learning.

Nurturing welcoming schools, No. 4: Facilitate less restrictive, more fluid classrooms

Whether in gifted and talented, mainstream, special education, or intentionally all-inclusive classes, Autistic students need opportunities to progress, as well as consistent, tailored support where appropriate, to facilitate their learning and enable them to succeed. As we have seen with extremely stressed-out straight-A student Cordeiro (they/them) above, there is more to flourishing in school than good grades. Vu (he/him) gives a great example of how the interrelated, complementary tools of continuous growth and support can be extended to any classroom context:

> One thing that would help would be to have special education courses be less restrictive on what individual students in the program can do. Some students naturally can learn faster than others and, thus, deserve a chance to move up and advance. If they advance to the point where they can take on regular classroom material, they should be able to do so while still having access to essential resources (such as speech therapy, counseling) if they need them. Access to such resources shouldn't disappear the moment a student...fully transitions into regular classroom settings.

A fluid, less restrictive approach may also entail letting students use fidgets, move their bodies in place, or even shift from one space to another. Benhamou (NP) explains that they would have benefited from the "freedom to leave the classroom and go to safer places," since being forced to stay in one place was "catastrophic...[while] not sitting in the classroom was good for me."

Additionally, students suffer when relegated to separate "special ed" classrooms. Bridge (they/them) decries the very real perils of rigid segregation, from othering to racism:

> [My school] was awful at disabilities. There was a segregated disability classroom that no one ever interacted with. They'd sometimes sit out in the halls and we'd stare at them and they'd stare at us. Special ed classrooms are not effective and are harmful to disabled students who get stuck there. Special ed classrooms are, additionally, spaces where black and brown students can disappear because of racism.

Meeting students where they are is a fundamental aspect of nurturing their intellectual and personal growth and development. Making room for them to thrive among their peers is also key. And being able to set one's own learning pace as a member of an inclusive student body is often crucial for students who learn differently. Incorporating and advocating for these flexible, student-centered approaches to learning—and offering and calling for ample, ongoing opportunities for both growth and support—can promote greater student satisfaction, achievement, and engagement, along with well-earned confidence.

Nurturing welcoming schools, No. 5: Organize regular one-on-one time with teachers

According to some of our survey respondents, time spent with teachers without the distractions of other students and hectic classroom environments can be highly beneficial. Personalized attention, offered in a less sensorially and interpersonally challenging context, can help Autistic students divide assignments into manageable chunks, develop and focus on timelines and goals, improve executive function, concentrate, feel included and connected, and more.

One respondent (she/her) recommends "organizing one-to-one time with people with learning disabilities so that they can learn better, as autistic people have different forms of learning in comparison to neurotypical people." Another respondent (she/her) also sees such individualized attention as a key accommodation: "I advocated very hard to get more accommodations without a formal diagnosis beyond 'gifted.' It was invalidating, but I got access to an alternative workspace and to one-on-one meetings with teachers to break down assignments."

Office hours, study halls/periods, flex blocks, or after-school

availability can provide opportunities for one-on-one attention from teachers, as another respondent (she/her) notes:

> At boarding school, each subject had after-school drop-in
> sessions. I attended them most weeks and that really helped
> with my learning as I cannot contain or learn everything at
> once in a classroom, and they help with homework... I did
> have a teacher though who was proactive, and if there was
> something I was not good at, he would look it up himself
> and help me. He would not let me move on until I got a
> question right or knew what it was.

Meeting one-on-one can also allow students and teachers to
find ways to work with more individualized subject matter that
speaks to each student's particular strengths and interests.

Clearly, caring and dedication are called for from all parties involved, since both teachers and students can feel overwhelmed by their regular school responsibilities. But in this
case, a little effort spent proactively can actually save a great
deal of time in the long run.

Nurturing welcoming schools, No. 6: Allow for looser deadlines/ more flexible schedules

Although every Autistic student has a unique learning style,
certain basic and very practical adaptations work well for many
and should be an integral part of any ND-friendly educational
environment. Plenty of other texts and materials cover specific
accommodations for Autistic learners in pedagogical settings
in great detail; we suggest referring to those suggestions
made—or at least fundamentally shaped by—Autistic people.

Here, we amplify the young Autistic voices and experiences
underlying the need for more flexible schedules and deadlines. And we highlight the fact that, as we expected, many of

our respondents expressed the view that taking an adaptive approach to time management is an absolutely crucial component of how inclusive schools can welcome neurodivergent students.

This can entail offering more time to finish tests; shortened assignments or assignments broken down into manageable, clear stages; tailored schedules and deadlines; and so on. As Ezra (he/him) suggests, "Being able to take things one step at a time would be helpful." "Gradual transitions" and "being able to take a lighter schedule" have also helped him.

One respondent (NP) outlines the benefits of taking the necessary time not only to complete but to fully understand school work:

> I take the same exams as some people in my year, and I can have special conditions. I get 30 minutes longer, and I can take breaks and go to the bathroom, and I have the exam in a different room because there's a lot of people in the hall... I get a special teacher. I take him the stuff I don't get from my other classes, and he helps me understand them.

One respondent (she/her) was diagnosed with ADHD prior to autism, but now notes that "I feel as though the accommodations given to those with ADHD can easily work for someone with ASD. I was given more time and a quiet testing area. It was very nice, and my grades improved."

Nurturing welcoming schools, No. 7: Offer alternative and adaptive supplies, materials, and environments

The previous sections are about welcoming rules and mindsets that enable students to learn at their own pace, while this section covers welcoming *things*, including educational tools as well as classroom and school environments. Things that can improve school success for Autistic students span the gamut from technologies that facilitate learning and communication to choosing—and, when possible, allowing students themselves to choose—compelling pedagogical materials. Marsh (they/them), for example, describes "becoming literate" only once they "discovered Star Wars Expanded Universe books." Bidon (she/her) says it's helpful when "they put on subtitles and captions in presentations." The key here is creating school environments where expressing and honoring each person's unique needs and abilities is an integral, ongoing practice.

Nonetheless, access to quiet spaces, whether for testing, learning, or self-regulation, is a fundamental educational need for most, if not all, Autistic young people. Several respondents describe quiet spaces as integral to learning. Kimble (she/her), for example, suggests, "There need to be designated quiet spaces for neurodivergent people to decompress because we get so overstimulated sometimes." Bidon (she/her) adds that she counts on such places for vital alone time, so she "can work more effectively." Forrester (any/varies) agrees, "I am an introvert, and interacting with people I don't know takes a lot of energy for me (although I enjoy it sometimes)."

Developing sensorially welcoming spaces is another central aspect of creating welcoming school communities. One respondent (she/her) says, "I wish school was a more sensory-friendly environment." For Corrado (she/her), a healthy learning environment is "one that is not sensory overloading." This can mean different strategies for different classrooms and students, but it's important to take steps toward sensory improvements and updates (there's lots more on these topics in general in Step 8). Fox (she/her) advises educators to start with some basic efforts: "When I think back, dimming the classroom lights slightly would have made a difference for me. Perhaps a good place to start is to trial small changes such as the lighting and see how they affect the students." Better yet, students and school staff can collaborate to determine which adaptations would be most helpful.

Nurturing welcoming schools, No. 8: Implement anti-bullying programs

Because students in these years are just discovering themselves, and therefore experimenting with power, relationships, morals, and more, middle and high school can be very challenging for young people of all neurologies. The sheer volume of experiences with bullies shared by our respondents is overwhelming and devastating. Perhaps more so than almost any other subgroup, Autistic students are profoundly vulnerable to this terrible treatment. One respondent (Hovet, she/her) even suggested requesting an autism assessment if you are being bullied (or your child is), since, in her experience, the students who get bullied the most/worst are the Autistic ones:

> Almost all autistic children experience bullying or rejection from peers on account of their autistic traits. Every single autistic person I know has experienced this, and so many personal accounts from autistic people include stories of bullying and abuse.

LGBTQIA+ and BIPOC Autistic youth endure even more abuse at the hands of their NT peers. ObeySumner (they/them) states, "Being a Black, autistic, femme, fat, and under-resourced person, I was automatically seen as someone—or something—to be attacked and exiled." Liu (she/her) explains, "At secondary school, boys would combine catcalling with racial harassment (e.g., slurs). Because I was autistic, I was more vulnerable to teasing and bullying, race-related or not." Nied (she/they) points to the painful repercussions of self-repression and masking that can arise from the fear of being bullied: "I remember really actively starting to suppress my stims in middle school so as not to draw attention to myself, which I already got plenty of for being a young queer kid in a conservative small town." One respondent (she/her), who is Asian, notes what a difference it made for her later in life when she found herself in an accepting environment where bullying was not tolerated, "The whole environment full of acceptance for diversity and empathy improved my mental condition so much."

McHugh (he/him) explores several aspects of neurodivergence that exacerbate the effects of bullying:

> There were issues with me when it came to working out whether someone might be serious or joking about something, since those with autism can find it difficult to work out voice tones and various forms of body language. I could also get confused if someone used complicated forms of language, particularly idioms.

Ksenhuk (he/him) observes that the "typical" tween/teen in the middle and high school years looks down on people who don't fit the "normal" mold: "It was very clear that there were people who don't accept anything that is different...they don't accept it, and they actually consider it a weakness." Raymond (he/him) experienced debilitating pain as a result of bullying:

> Because I was bullied in school nonstop, this only added to the damage and made me feel lesser about myself. I spent a grave chunk of my life being told that I was flawed and this condition defined my worth. It took a lot of introspection for me to finally realize I was a dope human being. No one had the right to tell me who I was or who I wasn't.

As just this small sample of quotes demonstrates, SCHOOLS MUST DO EVERYTHING IN THEIR POWER TO PROTECT AND INCLUDE ALL AUTISTIC STUDENTS.

What sorts of anti-bullying programs actually work? Our respondents suggest raising awareness about diversity with input and participation from representatives from a variety of marginalized groups. Comprehensive, school-wide bullying prevention trainings led by diverse professionals are a good place to start. But words alone may not be enough to deter bullying—Autistic and NT students, parents, educators, and others should integrate pro-inclusion/anti-bullying efforts into every area of the school experience, from curriculum to cultures, policies, and beyond. Hiring intersectional (ND, LGBTQIA+, BIPOC) leaders, employees, teachers, and presenters is another great way schools can help students see the humanity, merit, and unity of all people.

Inclusive school cultures value the inherent worth of all members and see differences as something to celebrate and incorporate into a vibrant and evolving learning process. And they have zero tolerance for bullying, period.

Nurturing welcoming schools, No. 9: Help people make friends when possible

Implementing strategies that help Autistic students connect with their peers is a proactive, if partial, remedy to the rampant bullying and alienation of Autistic middle and high school students. This starts with Autistic students believing in themselves and supporting each other, NT students allying with their ND peers, and teachers, staff, and parents actively encouraging participation and connection—all of which are more likely in schools that actively cultivate inclusivity.

School activities that facilitate personal achievements and promote positive relationships can lead naturally to friendship. For example, as one respondent (he/him) demonstrates, music classes and being in a band bring musical students together: "I didn't have many friends in high school, outside those in drumline. School would have been better if I'd had friends or activities to do that I liked."

Arts in general are a great subject to connect around. Gallant (she/her) describes how she was able to make friends once in a school where shared interests were celebrated:

For my sophomore year and the rest of my high school career, I transferred to an arts school where I was able to use my skills to show others what I am good at and passionate about. I became fixated on my arts goals and my social life greatly improved. I believe that allowing students to choose smaller charter and specialized schools would help the neurodiverse find a community they belong to through shared interest. My arts charter school saved my life.

Smaller group interactions are another way to encourage friendships, as in Nora's (she/her) school environment: "I guess I've never found it particularly hard to make friends, but I'd always gone to such small schools that I couldn't not be friends with everyone."

In any large or small school context—a gathering, recess, classroom, or other environment—Autistic students seeking positive interactions and connections may benefit from clarity around group focus and protocol. Bridge (they/them) notes that "I would have appreciated more structured, interest-oriented activities instead of being set loose to 'run around the playground.'" It's important, though, that any pro-friend activity, group, or meeting does not carry a stigma; that usually means attracting and integrating a diverse variety of both "typical" students and those with differences.

Nurturing welcoming schools, No. 10: Offer more inclusive after-school activities

As we've seen, many Autistic students appreciate some separation between academic and social pursuits, but they also may benefit from schools that provide opportunities to make friends in supportive, sensory-friendly, "discrimination-free" environments (anonymous, she/her). After-school activities can be the perfect solution.

To really serve students, however, after-school activities should proactively welcome all participants. Abramowski (she/her) says, "Inclusivity in extra-curriculars would invite students of all needs and abilities, and provide accommodations where needed." One respondent (he/him) outlines some key parameters: "They can make modifications to activities to allow everyone to participate fully, for example, time, location, intensity, type." Forrester (any/varies) adds, "They can welcome students who are non-speaking, and provide alternate ways of communication." Marsh (they/them) suggests that members and leaders "make sure the student is seen and heard." And Bidon (she/her) suggests letting people move around, rather than forcing them to stay in one place or sit still.

Moody (she/her) describes her vision of an ideal context:

> After-school activities should be adapted to be suited to [each] person's needs. A club should try to communicate with everyone in their own comfortable form, and it should be appreciative of each individual's talents and skills. For example, if one person is great at sewing, then that should be celebrated. Also, including visual symbols and photos along with the after-school activities [is helpful].

Sometimes things that seem obvious to NT students and staff can be baffling to Autistic students. "Clear communication" (Baik, she/her) is a huge part of this approach. For example, one respondent (she/her) notes that it is helpful when clubs and sports are clear about the expected experience level for participants.

One respondent (she/they) recommends both offering a broad selection of affinity and activity groups and ensuring that each has clear guidelines for interaction/play:

> I get very nervous when trying out new things. I think it would be easier for me if there were stronger guidance and a wider range of subjects to choose from. For example, I

really like Rubik's cubes, but it is difficult to find people who share that interest.

Schools can also help Autistic students by encouraging them to start their own groups based on their strengths and interests, and offering space and other resources to support them. As one respondent (she/her) advises, "Talk to your school office and see what needs to be done in order to create a club. Find a teacher who respects and understands you—they'll help you with the club."

Since Autistic students are often especially in need of opportunities to connect, Bridge (they/them) notes that it's important to "reduce costs for low-income students, [and] provide incentives for students who don't have the luxury to engage in unpaid activities." For the same reason, schools might also consider giving Autistic students the chance to sign up for clubs and groups before opening up enrollment. In one respondent's (she/her) words, "Give autistic people first priority in choosing activities so that they can choose ones that match their needs."

While many Autistic people experience motor and proprioceptive differences, some respondents suggested athletics as a way to be "successful" (Macedo, he/him), "gain respect" (Cohen, she/her), and connect. Making athletics fair and inclusive may take many forms, including, but not limited to, developing intramural sports teams, clubs, inclusive field days, or Unified Sports programs, and examining the exclusive culture that prevents people from even trying out for teams with limited rosters. All such efforts should explicitly "take into account that people may have coordination challenges" (Corrado, she/her) and/or other physiological differences, and aim diligently and continuously toward acceptance and adaptation. As Cordeiro (they/them) points out, inclusion in extracurriculars doesn't usually just happen on its own:

As someone with pretty noticeable dyspraxia, I felt left out in gym class. Teachers and students must make an active effort to include disabled peers, whether it be through altering the game or even having hard conversations about disability and how to be more inclusive.

This brings us to our final section about traditional schools.

Nurturing welcoming schools, No. 11: Teach students about disability

Jenny has always been baffled by the ways humans judge and exclude their fellow beings—and she doesn't think this "lack of understanding" is a "deficit"! Because she, along with most of her fellow Autistics, naturally operates from a more inclusive mindset, it took her decades to realize that many NT people engage better with people with differences when they know someone with those particular differences, or at least have *knowledge* about those differences. This is never more true than in middle and high school, which can be brutal for Autistic youth (and others, too).

In Moody's (she/her) view, we need to dismantle main-stream education's one-size-fits-all mentality, and its attempts to "fit everyone into boxes," so as to "help everyone learn to accept Autism and disabilities." But many respondents reported a dire lack of awareness in their schools. Kimble's (she/her) "high school didn't show that they accept everyone. They were very discriminating towards anyone who was different than the average person." One respondent (she/her) found that "the structure of the school system enforces and upholds ableism." Another respondent (she/her) decried her school's deficiencies in addressing certain forms of difference and disability:

Nothing is done to spread awareness and knowledge about [most] disabilities. They do teach us to be accepting of people who are "different," but I think that the students only interpret that as accommodating visible/noticeable disabilities. As my disability is not visible and I do quite a good job at hiding my autistic traits (or at least I think I do), people just see me as weird instead of disabled, and think that my different behaviour is voluntary.

Several (anonymous, she/her; Jo, she/her; Nora, she/her) mentioned that autism was never even discussed or mentioned at school. These sorts of ignorance can be debilitating for Autistic students.

Abramowski's (she/her) experience demonstrates the potential benefits for all students—disabled or not—of a curriculum that includes disability awareness and acceptance:

> I remember learning about various disabilities in school, before I was diagnosed with any myself. I feel that I learned about differences from an early age, and was always drawn to others with disabilities, as I found connection with them. Now I realize that this is because I have that in common with them!

Vu (he/him) suggests getting input from Autistic adults and others with differences:

> I think one way curricula could improve is by having testimonies from autistic or disabled adults or even inviting them to speak and talk to the class. As a child, I felt that it would've been valuable to have an autistic adult guide me through the motions and show me that my disability doesn't define my potential for success.

He adds that such programs allow us to transcend division by enabling him "and other students to accept autism and other disabilities." Vu believes these programs have helped "focus on key things that allow us to move past our social divides (race, gender, etc.) and focus on the human beings we are."

One respondent (she/her) describes the fundamental shift that can occur with deeper knowledge:

> When most people think of autism, they think of the Hollywood version. They do not think about the computer engineer in the IT department who has a wife and kids. They don't think about the quiet librarian at the public library. The only thing that neurotypicals know is that you are violating some unknown code. Many of them do not even understand why they dislike you, but they do. But sometimes, something suddenly clicks. And their dislike of you can turn into understanding.

Autistic students deserve schools that put the necessary effort into disability/difference education, awareness, and acceptance so that this crucial "click" is more likely to occur. They have the right to attend schools where there is, in Cordeiro's (they/them) words, "zero tolerance for any type of discrimination. (They also must actively fight it)." Students, families, educators, therapists, and others who see the value in uplifting and educating all students via disability awareness and acceptance can learn from these suggestions and follow through with concrete actions. In these ways, we can make our schools into spaces "that value empathy over bullying" (Harrington, she her).

OTHER EDUCATIONAL SETTINGS

Nurturing welcoming schools, No. 12: Vocational programs and schools

Students, families, and educators/therapists/staff at *any* type of school can advocate for implementing the preceding suggestions for improving schools for Autistic tweens and teens. But vocational schools may also offer several unique advantages over typical school settings. Since Autistic students often struggle to connect with their peers, the shared interests reflected in vocational training serve to foster relationships grounded in genuine communication and learning. These schools and programs also offer career preparation and practical skills, which is why education professionals increasingly support them—and why students of all neurologies are turning to these valuable institutions (Chen, 2022).

Vocational schools and programs offer a variety of practical, hands-on, real-life classes, from cosmetology to culinary arts, and automotive repair to programming and web development. One respondent (NP) believes learning these kinds of skills could make all the difference for Autistic youth. They suggest it would be helpful for Autistic people, as well as those with other disabilities, to have access to more job training and work opportunities. In their view, programs that educate and enable disabled people to drive, support themselves financially, and live independently would also be beneficial.

Vocational programs and schools also give students the chance to explore career possibilities, a key aspect of education, according to Max (he/him):

> One of the biggest challenges I faced transitioning into young adulthood was figuring out what sort of jobs I enjoyed. I was fortunate enough to get a job as a food service worker at a high school three months after graduating, and I love what I do, and still work there after four years, but I feel there should be more opportunities for young adults to explore what fields of work they might enjoy.

Vocational schools and programs can offer some of these practical and career-oriented benefits, while also evolving their environments and practices to be more inclusive following the general school-related suggestions offered above.

Nurturing welcoming schools, No. 13: Homeschooling

While homeschooling differs in several obvious ways from other school settings, many elements of the above guidelines can be usefully integrated into homeschool contexts. Home-schooled students and their teachers, families, advocates, and allies should definitely also take a close look at Step 1 (Foster Inclusive, Accepting Family Dynamics and Homes), since academics are just one of many challenging aspects of growing up and learning—and a welcoming home environment can be all the more crucial in the homeschool context.

Certain features unique to homeschooling can be perfectly suited to some Autistic learners. For one thing, homeschooling can be ideal for integrating interest spikes. It also allows students to focus on academics without social distractions. And it can facilitate a more sensorially supportive and welcoming environment. Corrado (she/her), for example, was homeschooled throughout her middle and high school years because she found regular school so overwhelming that she would "hide in the library." As a bonus, students with close connections to their animal companions can rely on that comfort and companionship at home.

But homeschooling may not provide crucial access to peers, so care should be taken to present opportunities to interact, whether via online connections, in real-life meetups, sports, gatherings, or clubs, or in libraries or other community spaces. When this aspect of learning is addressed, homeschooled students may actually find that they are better able to practice autism-friendly modes of interaction than their peers at brick-and-mortar schools.

Conclusion: Doing what it takes to improve middle and high school for Autistic students

As we have seen, the middle and high school years can be especially rough on Autistic youth. Some are able to turn that adversity into extraordinary advocacy and other successes. Chen (she/her), for instance, used her experiences to fuel her passion for advocacy:

> I told my teachers and "came out" as autistic entirely on social media with the utter joy of finally being able to live as who I am, but the reaction I received was a cold, hard slap of reality on my face. The teachers who ignored my emails, friends who wouldn't meet me in the eye, and people who told me that they were "sorry for me"...these hurt. However, I am also thankful for these torturous experiences as they inspired an advocacy project I initiated with the team at *Detester Magazine* to improve autistic accessibility in schools.

Raymond (he/him) also turned pain into action, in his case through writing:

> Due to bullying and the circumstances I was forced to cope with, it beat me down terribly. It was through my suffering that I discovered I had a passion for writing. So I used the stones I had tossed at me to build an empire with. I soon became unstoppable. Now, writing books has enabled me to branch out. I started performing spoken word, creating music, making films, and creating content for social media just by expressing my true and authentic self. I have developed a new-found sense of confidence. I became more spiritual in the process as well.

Both Raymond (he/him) and Chen (she/her) are amazing examples of Autistic human resilience and inner strength. But their victories do not excuse a laissez-faire attitude toward inclusion.

As the many difficult experiences shared in this step demonstrate, schools must learn to support and include all students. Autistic tweens and teens, their families, educators, and anyone else involved can work to evolve middle and high school environments via the above recommendations—and thereby create schools that actually promote healthy growth, connection, and learning for all.

SUMMARY GUIDANCE:
#ActuallyAutistic practical tips for school

- Schools must openly discuss, celebrate, and adapt to differences early and often; families can help by sharing and exploring diagnoses with children (including newly diagnosed tweens and teens) from the outset.
- Promote autism understanding in school communities via clear, positive information, workshops, clubs, and so on.
- Ensure that teachers are both aware and accepting of neurodiversity.
- Advocate for flexible, open classroom inclusion policies and assignment deadlines.
- Consider alternative class/group sizes (including regular one-on-one teacher–student meetings) and subjects of study.
- Brainstorm ways to include different needs and abilities in communication, sensory, movement, learning, social/interactive, and other contexts.
- Include Autistic adults as role models, leaders, teachers, and anti-bullying/pro-neurodiversity advocates.
- Remember that alternative modes of education, such as vocational schools/programs, charter, independent,

or magnet schools, and homeschooling, may offer certain advantages for Autistic students. When such options are inaccessible, consider integrating autism-friendly aspects of alternative learning practices, such as smaller classes or focused, tailored activities.

- Develop/advocate for extracurricular activities that welcome and serve a range of students.

REFLECTION QUESTIONS

? Are you doing what you can to support effective, enjoyable modes of learning for yourself and/or the Autistic person/people in your life?

? Is welcoming diversity built into every level of your school, including curriculum, culture, and so on? How can schools foster harmony and resilience in diverse populations?

? How can you better connect with others, and help Autistic students do so?

? Are you aware of your's and others' coordination, motor skills, proprioception, and other physical differences, and do you insist on adaptive solutions for inclusion?

? What would improve your/your child's/client's/ students' classroom/learning experience? Consider implementing sensory updates, creating quiet spaces, developing clear boundaries between, academic and social activities, breaking projects down into clear, manageable steps, and other Step 4 suggestions.

? How can you help to create conditions at school that both welcome all neurologies and adapt to particular needs?

? What strategies would be truly effective against bullying in your school? How can you support implementation?

? Does your school offer a range of adaptive learning supplies, spaces, materials, and technologies?

Advocating for Inclusive Transitions to Adulthood

Navigating the shift from childhood to adult life is a challenge for most humans, especially those with neurological differences and disabilities. This is not because of any failing on their part, but because the mainstream world—from housing and work to the sensory environment—is set up for neurotypical people. This stage offers neuro-affirmative, informed, proactive tips for making these transitions more fair, enjoyable, and successful for Autistic young people.

Step 5

Navigate the Transition Out of High School

Going from a place I have lived for the past 15 years and where I have a cemented morning and evening routine to suddenly a whole new environment where I am no longer surrounded by my family—who are essentially my comfort blanket—was one of the hardest things I have ever done... However, it has also been one of the most rewarding.

—FOX (SHE/HER)

Transitions can cause a wide range of emotions, from anxiety and stress to excitement and relief. This is especially true for many Autistic people, who may find change hard in general. And it's true for all post-high school transitions, including, but not limited to, choosing and beginning to participate in college, internships, work-training programs, trade schools, supported living, independent living, volunteering, part- or full-time work, and gap years between work and school. To facilitate smooth transitions, self-advocates can gain confidence with thorough planning before and during each transition, and being gentle with themselves through this significant period of change. Allies must develop an inclusive mindset necessary for advocating with those they care about. This step is devoted to this important in-between time—how to decide what's next and how to prepare for that transition, whatever it may look like.

Navigating the transition out of high school, No. 1: Decide on next steps

Why is this needed?

There is no one-size-fits-all track after high school. What worked for a parent, older sibling, or older relative, or what is currently planned for a peer, is not necessarily indicative of what should happen with someone else's life. Self-advocates can absorb the options, take an inventory of what they need and want, and plan accordingly. Allies can offer suggestions and help their loved ones figure out what's next, with the understanding that we each have our own path. The suggestions below describe ways to help you start the process of sorting out the various possibilities and assessing which paths are the best fit (for yourself or a loved one).

Offering choices and opportunities

Marsh (they/them) says they both dreaded and anticipated adulthood, hoping that it would be less oppressive. Marsh insists that "the only way to ease the transition is to let the autistic person define it." It's helpful if high schools are able to encourage and support students in career exploration. Some schools will emphasize that all students should follow a path to college, isolating those who don't end up pursuing higher education. Others may, sometimes unintentionally, tend to relegate students with differences to vocational paths or limited "special ed" courses/tracks, without letting them initiate or choose their own trajectories. Vu (he/him) says he wishes his high school had encouraged students to explore their interests and career paths "rather than simply feed them down the college pipeline (which doesn't work for everyone)":

Not everyone knows what they want to do after high school, and it can be stressful to figure that out while you're trying to get through high school (academically and socially). Perhaps, schools could have classes or special programs where people could learn vocational or trade skills (such as welding, dentistry) or even do projects in a field they're interested in.

Career and college exploration is often initiated or encouraged by school counselors, but is sometimes in conflict with student desires. One respondent (NP) describes their experience with a common manifestation of this conflict as being discouraged from following one's dreams because one might not seem to have the "right" qualifications for a typical route to those dreams. They explain, "I want to go to university and study geology or astronomy, but my counselor says I should go to adult education to learn life skills and how to take care of myself, and that I don't have university grades."

To truly support students through this period, teachers, counselors, therapists, and other professionals working with diverse populations in high schools should educate themselves around helping all students work toward their own goals in their own ways, rather than forcing them on a set path determined by neuro-normalized expectations or blanket policies. And Autistic students, along with their families and other allies, should bear in mind that there are many routes to achieving their goals. We all have strengths and something to offer.

Bridge (they/them) says their social workers helped them understand their potential:

We need people who won't try and funnel black and brown kids to athletics and nursing. We need people who believe that disabled and BIPOC kids have potential and can do great things with their lives. It was the belief of all the social workers in my life that I could amount to something that let me be who I am today.

Navigating the possibilities of life after high school (or helping someone you care about do so) must begin with an affirmation of self-worth, a belief in all human potential, and the courage to resist stereotyped paths that don't seem like a good fit.

Having a flexible schedule

Life after high school often fosters independence, opening paths to pursue varied interests of one's own choosing. Not all paths will be fruitful, but with some patience we can find or help someone else find meaningful options. People also might have the opportunity for a more flexible schedule after high school, as they choose between post-secondary school, work experience, or other options. Some Autistic people may find the new lack of structure (compared to a clearly delineated high school schedule) challenging; others may welcome this shift. Balfour (she/her) says that "going forward, something that will really help in my career will be the ability to set my own schedule and have flexible hours." One respondent (she/her) hopes that the next campus she will be attending is smaller and easier to navigate.

Choosing a backup plan can help make sure that you stay in control of your life even when things don't go perfectly. One respondent (she/they) shares their post-high school plans as well as a backup plan: "I would like to study medicine at university, but I am not sure if I will get in. If I don't, my backup plan is to do a year of volunteer work in a hospital and then try again."

Sometimes taking some time off from school is needed. Marsh (they/them) says that they held off on enrolling in further studies because of concerns about test-taking and academic writing. One respondent (she/her) says she is planning on working and saving for a year before applying for classes at a university. She explains, "This way I can focus on my first-year studies without getting a job at the same time."

Gradual changes are best where possible. Slowly changing life variables can make post-high school transitions a bit smoother. And building flexibility into the schedule can create opportunities to pursue varied interests and help with managing the workload.

Understanding it's okay to keep figuring it out

While planning for the future can potentially alleviate anxiety during transitions, it's also okay to give yourself (or the one you care about) some grace and understand that finding what works best is an ongoing process. Often, people start with entry-level or volunteer work positions while they search for something that better suits their interests or skills. Some people choose to work and attend school part time while they consider how much they enjoy specific classes. Others need space and time away from traditional post-secondary school settings to consider their next steps. And sometimes paths that are initially chosen end up not being a good fit at that particular time, forcing people to choose a new path or try again with new supports or under different conditions.

Several respondents shared ambivalence about their futures. Williams (he/him) says, "I am currently not working a part-time job, but want to be doing more volunteer opportunities in my community." One respondent (she/her) says that while she likes school, she has grown tired of it. But she finds the job-application process frustrating:

> Applying to jobs can be difficult for me because I don't always understand the language that they're using in the application when they ask questions about me. I wish I had a better sense of self, because I feel like that would allow me to find what makes me happy for longer terms.

Some respondents remained positive despite not knowing what would come next. Kimble (she/her) explains, "I'm currently working at Texas Roadhouse and I plan to stay there for a while before hopefully getting a job at the hospital." Ernesto (he/him) also remains hopeful for the future. "I've worked a few times, and I failed out of college, but after a while, I think I'll get on my feet."

Navigating the transition out of high school, No. 2: Utilize disability/transition services

Why is this needed?

There are many different structural supports for people transitioning out of high school, but according to our respondents, there is room for improvement. Service quality and types will vary internationally and even within local regions, so it's important for Autistic people to start researching what is available in their area and begin applying for services they might need, if appropriate.

Our respondents' comments highlight both the importance of quality transition services and where gaps exist. Marsh (they/them) says the available services post-high school "fail miserably." Maclean (NP) explains, "Here in New Zealand we've got a long way to go for people who are autistic as they're still exclusive about schooling, employment, and more." In Kronby's (they/them) experience, "There are a lot of programs for grade school, but universities are largely lacking inclusion programs based on neurodiversity."

A lack of support can have serious consequences on life trajectories. Chloe (she/her) says she had to drop out of college because of a lack of diagnosis and supports. Cleaver (she/her) compares her experience pursuing two degrees, one with support and one without, "The one I did with help is a first, despite it being more academically intensive. Unfortunately, since then the quality and quantity of help available has declined." Our contributors countered these negative experiences with helpful anecdotes of what was working and ideas for change.

Finding helpful resources, including peer mentorship and social supports

Kronby (they/them) suggest that "student advocates and peer mentorship" in schools can ease transitions. Peer mentors familiar with how disabilities services work at the university level can share tips and insights. Kronby say they appreciate that their disability services center has been accessible:

> They answer your calls and emails, even if things don't run smoothly. The manager of the program has been communicative and is the reason our accommodations request even went to the dean for review. We have heard much worse stories from others and their university's practices. We have been lucky to not share their horrendous experiences.

Some people need support seeking and maintaining social relationships in school and in the workplace, as Oesterle (she/they) points out:

> It has been really hard to connect with my peers in graduate school. Work has always been manageable, but I struggled with connecting to my co-workers a lot, especially when things like Happy Hour come up. I have some health needs that need to be taken care of in the morning, so it is hard to request accommodations without feeling like I am being lazy! It has been the first time I have registered with disability, too, because I was ashamed.

Oesterle suggests that "more awareness of sensory differences and communication issues would be helpful," but realizes she also needs to use her voice to self-advocate. "This is a really hard area for me because I love what I do and just struggle a lot with the social norms of a workplace."

Securing housing programs, disability benefits, and other accommodations

Education and other accommodations after high school were mixed for our respondents. Some respondents were satisfied with or optimistic about the supports they received/planned on receiving and others were disappointed and had cautionary tales to consider when planning for future accommodations. For example, one respondent (she/her) says that finding somewhere to live was very hard. Supportive housing programs may have long waiting lists and/or stringent requirements, while exploring resources and strategies for living on your own has its own set of challenges (discussed in more detail in Step 6).

Marsh (they/them) appreciated that their parents had the forethought to get them on Supplementary Security Income (SSI) before they finished their BA. Day (e/em/eir) expressed frustration with the social expectations within the academic setting that some professors require and the general access barriers to obtaining the proper supports in this setting. "When I'm non-verbal or can't socialize my point correctly, I get graded worse." Day explains what happens if e wants note-taking assistance:

> I have to have an in-depth evaluation of my current capabilities, but there are very few doctors' places that will provide these tests. This requires a big trip and usually costs a lot between the gas, taking time off work, copays for an out-of-network doctor, and so on. So I don't qualify for assistance from the school.

If you or the person you care about are having trouble accessing disability transition services or question the adequacy of systems currently in place, there are more in-depth resources available. The Autistic Self Advocacy Network (ASAN) has published several guides for young adults to help navigate transitions out of high school and access and advocate for much-needed supports:

- The *Navigating College: A Handbook on Self Advocacy* guide has tips for students trying to secure housing and educational accommodations.
- *Accessing Home and Community-Based Services: A Guide for Self-Advocates* is a guide to help people learn about housing rights, housing vouchers, and community-living options.
- *Roadmap to Transition: A Handbook for Autistic Youth Transitioning to Adulthood* helps people make transitional plans and discusses self-determination, self-advocacy, post-secondary employment, healthcare, housing, and more.

Navigating the transition out of high school, No. 3: Expect a mixture of relief, excitement, and fear

Why is this needed?
New life-changing decisions can often trigger conflicting emotions, all of which are equally valid. If we understand this, we can better manage these emotions and not give too much weight to one over another in our decision-making process. Our respondents experienced fear, anxiety, excitement, pride, and relief during the transition out of high school. Being aware that each of these emotions is natural and felt by many will help Autistic students and those who care for them prepare for their transitions.

Understanding that fear and anxiety are common
Many respondents said they were scared about the transition out of high school. Some of this fear came from what they had been told by others about this stage of their lives. One respondent (she/her) says, "more information and fewer scare tactics (i.e., 'your professors in university won't be so accepting')" would have made her feel more comfortable. Harrington

(she/her) had a similar experience: "The adults lied. They made my high school life hell and said this was the happiest I'd ever get. Life post-high school was not nearly as terrifying as they made it out to be."

Others mentioned the difficulty of entering a new place where they wouldn't know anyone. One respondent (NP) admits, "I don't want to know different people," and another respondent (she/they) shares that she is "afraid that I won't find any friends there, and that the busy environment could be overwhelming." Vu (he/him) explains that he felt a mixture of relief and fear:

> On one hand, I felt relieved to be leaving high school as, despite the good memories I had there, it was, in a sense, a reminder of the trauma, sexual harassment, and the social disconnection I experienced there. On the other, I felt confused, lost, and unsure of myself as many of my peers were headed off to the military, trade school, college, and other post-secondary career routes.

Lessard (she/her) says she was "incredibly homesick" during the college transition and only felt adjusted after about two-and-a half years. For Lessard, the most challenging part was being away from home and her close-knit familial support system, "I think it got easier for me once I learned to treat college as something that was simply part of my routine, and pushed myself to make connections with people on campus so I wouldn't feel quite so isolated." In her experience:

> College represented a huge step outside of my comfort zone. To this day, I massively prefer my school breaks spent at home and my weekend visits during semesters to the time I spend on campus. This isn't because of disliking my school; I very much feel that my school is the best place for me in terms of my education, and I've learned to be quite happy there.

Sometimes the anxiety comes from the uncertainty about the options available and what might come next. One respondent (she/they) says, "I am a bit scared. I particularly fear the uncertainty about what will happen after graduation, so I wish there were more transition services and help when applying for university."

Families of Autistic youth must find a balance between learning about and sharing possible options for the future while being careful not to evoke even more anxiety with warnings of higher expectations and new demands. And Autistic young people can give themselves some time to understand that their different and sometimes contradictory emotions are normal and to work through all of the questions about what is to come.

Remembering there is also much to be relieved and excited about, and even proud of

While fear and anxiety are common during this transition, there are plenty of positives, too. Baik (she/her) says she felt relieved at her graduation ceremony because she "finally got through what were the most difficult six years of my life." She says the best part of life post-high school is "the independence and flexibility... I'm not bound by four walls seven hours a day like I was at high school." One respondent (she/they) is hopeful that the topics in college will be more interesting since they get to choose their course of study. Forrester (any/varies) was worried about finding good friends, but says, "As it turned out, that was not a problem."

Some respondents were proud of their post-high school decisions. Lessard (she/her) says, "At college, I've thrived in my studies, as well as become involved in extracurriculars and built a small social life. These are things I never thought I would be capable of, so that's something extremely rewarding for me."

Fox (she/her) explains that the most challenging part of life after high school is the change, but she appreciates the independence and has confidence in her ability to manage things on her own. She also has a support system she can access when she struggles:

> I also have a loving, patient, and supportive partner who helps me through when difficulties present themselves... There are still days where I struggle, so I will go and visit my parents and brother. Even sitting with them for half an hour can make all the difference to my mental state; it recharges me better than anything else can.

Fox (she/her) advises anyone else moving out of their family home to "take it one step at a time": "It is a big change for anybody, not just those with ASD, so don't put too much pressure on yourself, and remember to stop and ask for support if you feel you need it."

Many other contributors recommended maintaining relationships with supportive family and friends to help with the transition. In Baik's (she/her) words, "What helps me through is the amazing people in my life." Bridge (they/them) says, "I was very fortunate that I had the support of community folks and social workers. I was okay because I had people who supported my dreams and goals and helped me strategize how to get there." Josey (he/him) says that supportive people help with these challenging transitions and new "colossal responsibilities" in a world that is "very cruel." He suggests, "What would make it better is if I just got some extra encouragement and support from people who love me. I don't want to give up on myself as they haven't given up on me." Others also spoke about the tragedy of not finding the proper support they needed.

The post-high school transition becomes easier when we acknowledge that the road may be unclear, bumpy, and not without twists and turns. But the opportunities of a new life after high school are also exciting and attainable—and become more so when informed by autism-friendly insights and planning.

Navigating the transition out of high school, No. 4: Keep in mind that available supports and support needs may shift

Why is this needed?

It's healthy to realize that both what supports are available and which supports are necessary or helpful for a given person may change after high school. That awareness can ensure you retain the confidence to continue self-advocacy and are prepared for changing routines and expectations. In some instances, a person's needs will change in different environments, or as that person grows and develops. In other situations, people may need to adjust to different expectations in the institutions and environments around them, whether in a college, workplace, training program, living arrangement, or any other new context. Knowing this will hopefully encourage the inquiry, introspection, and self-discovery necessary for ongoing self-advocacy in a variety of different environments and stages of life. These learning practices, particularly having an inquiring mindset, are also useful for genuinely helpful advocacy and allyship.

Being aware that scaffolding or structure might be needed to support new executive functioning demands

Several respondents mentioned difficulty with juggling new demands in new situations. Balfour (she/her) explains, "Once I didn't have an external structure to follow, I started to really struggle with executive dysfunction." Macedo (he/him) was fortunate enough to have peer support during adolescence, but says that as an adult:

I find myself having to accommodate the rest of the world a lot more in terms of adhering to social systems and more collective expectations. An example would be accommodating others by having your work email be the main form of communication, instead of your work phone, which may be more manageable and less of a hassle.

Macedo notes that it's "increasingly challenging to balance 'soft tasks,' such as gathering documents together, and working on multiple tasks at once."

Hall (she/her) says:

The concept of going to university is terrifying, as change always is... The problem with being my age is that things change all the time. One minute I'm in high school struggling to concentrate on exams as my OCD [obsessive compulsive disorder] gets worse and the next I've left school and am working as a waitress dealing with new and complicated situations. Things are not the same anymore after leaving high school, and I fear that if I put too much pressure on myself, I'll crack, and if I don't push myself enough, I'll crumble.

If you are an Autistic person navigating the transition out of high school, give yourself time and grace to figure out what your new needs are. Know that others have encountered these challenges, and that there are ways to scaffold yourself, as well as resources to aid in doing so. A big part of the end of high school and early post-high school life is figuring out what those needs and resources might be—and following through on them at your own pace. Online tools are increasingly available for time and task management—and some, such as Goblin Tools (https://goblin.tools), are geared toward neurodivergent people. These can help with the many new transitions, obligations, and skills inherent in this time of life. If you absolutely must work or start college on a certain timeline, look for ways to build in rest and activities that strengthen your resilience and conserve (or even add to) your spoons.

Navigating the transition out of high school, No. 5: Know that post-high school activities may entail higher or different expectations

Why is this needed?

According to what many of our respondents anticipated or experienced, post-high school activities may require more intense expectations. One respondent (he/him) mentions harder material. Baik (she/her) says the coursework can be "so tedious" and "more challenging than what you learn at high school." Understanding and preparing for this possibility will hopefully help prevent situations like Kimble's (she/her) "horrible" community college experience: "It absolutely wrecked my mental health, to a point where I had to be hospitalized twice. So I left college. It wasn't worth it."

Trying not to compare yourself to peers

When we try to meet the new bar that we or others set for us (or we are setting for the people we care about), remember that everyone is unique, so peer comparisons generally aren't very helpful. Cordeiro (they/them) explains their experience has been "slower-paced than the majority of my peers, but I hope to make a difference in the lives of people like me." If you or someone you care about has a high school graduation looming, remember that the next path (or your child/friend/student/client/relative's, and so on) is your/their own. Don't judge yourself or others too harshly for navigating this period in different ways, whether that means moving through stages in longer or shorter periods of time than your peers, or accessing more or fewer supports than those around you.

Navigating the transition out of high school, No. 6: Think about joining a social support group

Why is this needed?

Social support groups can offer all kinds of crucial benefits for life after high school. They help form friendships, offer opportunities for connections with like-minded people, and widen support systems once daily attendance in school with peers is no longer required. Good friendships can also help curb loneliness, isolation, and depression. A social support group doesn't have to be explicitly labeled as such—it could be a club, get-together, or activity focused on something you are interested in or love doing, or even a regular outing with someone or a group of people. The people we surveyed shared how important it was to have a regular, socially supportive activity or gathering they were comfortable with so they could be themselves and connect with others.

Having an outlet to be yourself and connect with others

Vu (he/him) said that social support groups would have been beneficial for him, especially during COVID. These groups allow people to:

> ...come together and just talk about themselves and have a safe space to express themselves fully without judgment and with an open mind and heart. Some people just need to vent about their problems (although only through healthy ways without death threats or violence) or are just lonely.

Vu believes this sort of setting would help people "of all walks of life."

Oesterle (she/they) had trouble identifying with her peers growing up and suggests that being a part of a community of Autistic people might have helped. Since they didn't share typical gendered interests, and mostly connected with male friends until adolescence, their female peer friendships were awkward, and Oesterle experienced social isolation. In their view, "I am not sure what could make this better other than having a community of autistic kids." Cleaver (she/her) says she struggled socially after her transition to university: "I could do the academic work, but my social skills were non-existent. I failed to make friends and ultimately barely scraped through my first degree." All of this points to the importance of "finding 'your people'" during this sensitive and sometimes difficult life transition. We suggest taking a closer look at Steps 2 and 3 for help with making and strengthening social connections during this crucial period.

Conclusion: Finishing high school with confidence and clarity

The guidance in this Step reflects the fears, insights, and experiences of Autistic young people dealing with the major shifts that occur at the end of high school. This transition will look different for every Autistic person, but the knowledge that there are things that will help can ease some of the harder aspects of leaving high school and boost the potential gains in self-determination. Integrating these #ActuallyAutistic perspectives can enable young Autistic people to embark on their own path uplifted by the wisdom of people who have shared similar challenges and successes.

SUMMARY GUIDANCE:
#ActuallyAutistic practical tips for the transition out of high school

- Let the Autistic person define their transitions out of school.

- Challenge career path/next step recommendations that seem limiting.
- Have a backup plan.
- When possible, limit the number of variable changes and favor gradual shifts.
- Give yourself (or the person you care about) grace and time to figure out next steps.
- If applying for college, inquire about disability services available at different schools.
- Research community-based disability transition services.
- Join clubs or social support groups focused on shared interests.
- Avoid making comparisons with others about your/ their life paths.
- Acknowledge the challenges, but remain optimistic about the future.
- Be aware that it's common for support needs to shift. Find a trusted person you (or the person you care about) can talk to about this if you (they) notice a need for different or additional accommodations.

REFLECTION QUESTIONS

? What am I (or is my loved one) most passionate about? What are the next steps to making this dream a reality?

? What is the backup plan?

? What do I (or does my loved one) perceive as the biggest obstacle to achieving my (their) goals post-high school?

? How will I (or my loved one) maintain friendships after high school or meet new people?

? In what ways do I need to take care of myself (or my loved one) during the next phase of life until a new routine is established?

? Have I reached out to counselors, social workers, local, state, and federal disability service programs to see what is available?

? When have I (myself, or as a parent/relative/friend/teacher/professional) made comparisons to others' paths as a way of learning (or teaching my child/relative/friend/student/client) about the future? In what ways was this helpful or unhelpful?

Step 6

Consider the Factors Involved in Early Independence

What I feel is important for adulthood is everyone should be capable of being fully independent.

—WILLIAMS (HE/HIM)

Why are these factors so important?

Autistic young adults often face more adulthood transition barriers than their peers. For one, not everything in the NT world is as obvious to Autistic people as it is to NTs. That's one of the main reasons we thought that factors involved in early independence would be a vital topic to cover extensively in this book! This chapter discusses a range of things that need to be considered and addressed when taking those first steps toward autonomy. For example, we talk about developing financial literacy, because this tool can boost your ability to make your own decisions by enabling you to manage your money so that you can do and buy the things you want (freedom!) and need (personal responsibility!). When neurodivergent youth have the information they need, they can make better choices, prioritize more effectively, and become more likely to achieve their goals. As Williams (he/him) implies above, independence is a *right*—one that knowledge and appropriate support can make possible in diverse ways for diverse people.

These transitions to adulthood can be stressful. We want to encourage Autistic youth and those who care about them to engage in as much self-care and stress-reduction as possible as they journey toward their independence goals and dreams. This might include seeing an autism-friendly or Autistic therapist (see Stage Four, our online resource on the Jessica Kingsley website, for tips on finding such therapists), leaning on/being a supportive family (Step 1), regular physical exercise, yoga, or dance, or anything else that feels soothing and healthy. For some, such as Phillips (NP) and Logan P. (prefers not to use pronouns), faith is a nourishing and uplifting facet of life. Logan P. explains:

> When I become more dependent on God instead of systems and circumstances, I find I'm more independent [myself], but I can also relate more to the essence in each person being made in the image of God. I don't have to rely on other people's emotions to know I have worth and that trust in God makes it easier to be independent without fear but still resilient in hardships.

Being proactive about mental and physical health can help you self-regulate, better achieve your objectives, and enjoy life more.

For many Autistic people entering young adulthood, the choice whether or not to apply for your country's disability support program is a complicated one (it could probably take up a whole book in itself!). This process usually occurs around the age of 18, and has been covered in the previous chapter (Step 5). The sections in this step regard going to college, working (including volunteering, training, interning, apprenticing, and so on), getting a driver's license/figuring out transportation, and living independently. These four aspects of young adulthood may overlap or may be pursued separately. In many instances, they are interrelated.

It's important to be aware that societal and legal supports do diminish in adulthood—as one respondent (she/her) notes, "There seems to be this never-ending support for children with disabilities, and yet the moment they turn 21, the support drops significantly." So one of the topics we will cover is accessing ongoing assistance as needed. Of course, while some Autistic young people will rely on public benefits and services, or other supports to progress toward their goals, others may simply need a bit more knowledge. We explore each of these transitions from the perspectives of our respondents, covering as many helpful details as possible in order to map out various possibilities—and suggest workarounds and solutions, where necessary.

Looking back while writing this book, Jenny realized there were quite a few aspects of independence she wasn't aware of and maybe could have handled better. For Step 6, we've aimed to touch on *all* of the key facets of moving into adulthood, so that Autistic readers can have at least some idea of where they may need to focus their energies. If you're dipping into this section rather than reading the book cover to cover, please be aware that Steps 5 and 7 cover some of the practical aspects of these shifts in greater detail.

Navigating early independence, No. 1: Choosing college

Deciding to pursue some form of higher education after high school is an option increasingly available to Autistic people, including those who experience learning differences. Many colleges and universities are actively recruiting Autistic students, and establishing offices of neurodiversity and the like, in order to enrich their student bodies and boost their inclusivity.

So students hoping to attend college should definitely look for those that have explicitly welcoming, encouraging cultures and offer a variety of academic assistance, where appropriate.

In countries where higher education is costly, paying for college can be a huge challenge and a barrier to attending. While this issue affects all students and is thus beyond the scope of this book, we did want to mention that many universities, countries, localities, organizations (such as vocational rehabilitation), and individuals offer scholarships and aid for students with disabilities and Autistic students.

Once they've selected some good possibilities for colleges to apply to and attend, Autistic students should determine two things. First, they must consider what sorts of academic, personal, and social needs they may have entering the college environment. Next, they must determine—honestly and thoughtfully—whether they will have the internal resources (or, in some cases, family or institutional support) to ensure that those needs are met.

These considerations are essential because support needs are handled very differently at the higher education level. In most high schools, academic support, adaptations, and modifications are mandatory and enforced. In college, students (and their families, if they have the students' permission) must communicate those needs, usually with institutional backup/"proof," such as a diagnosis, or, in the United States, an IEP or 504 plan from high school.

Once they've communicated those needs and arrived on campus, students themselves are also responsible for making sure they take advantage of whatever programs, resources, and supportive structures a college offers, which could include things like an office of academic support, peer tutoring program, wellness center, counseling, center for neurodiversity, and so on. In addition to offering supports around academics, executive function, mental health, and so on, these sites are also often good places to find a mentor, Autistic ally/friend, or other types of friends or allies who can offer encouragement, give tips for success, and help ease the challenges of college life.

Because most college students are adults, they are considered capable of making their own decisions, for better or worse. When students don't participate in necessary programs or access accommodations, it can impact academic success and other facets of college achievement, including mental health. For example, Bidon (she/her) says she was "left to my own devices to cope with meltdowns."

The good news is, many respondents found college more welcoming than high school. Moody (she/her) struggled in high school, "while my college I'm currently at helps people to learn to accept Autism and disabilities through teaching about them, encouraging discussion and learning." Baik (she/her) exults, "My university has been amazing in terms of understanding my neurodivergence." And Harrington (she/her) notes, "College and graduate school were much more accepting of me as a disabled person." Many respondents also really look forward to or appreciate having more freedom.

Still, there are many things to keep in mind during this transition. We suggest reading through this whole section prior to the application process, when possible. Autistic young people who intend to attend college may benefit from taking the following measures.

Preparing for new social challenges

New social environments can present significant difficulties for many Autistic people. Whether they experience internal or external pressure to mask, and/or feel awkward or overwhelmed when meeting new people, Autistic students starting college will have a lot to deal with in the interpersonal sphere. While less time spent with family or in the high school grind might feel like a relief for some, the opportunities for independence that come with college life can mean many feel isolated, especially at first. And all of that is on top of a whole new academic context.

On the plus side, college students are generally more mature and often more inclusive than younger people. For one respondent, among others, socialization improved after high school—but had its limits: "At uni, things are better and more inclusive towards me. But, people liked drinking, so I was rarely invited to parties. Other than that, people were generally nice to me." One respondent (she/her) thrived academically, but "experienced some social difficulties."

Lessard (she/her) details a number of areas in which Autistic college students may benefit from self-advocacy "in social settings":

> I've grown more comfortable with actually disclosing that I'm autistic to my friends and acquaintances when it becomes relevant. I've removed myself from a few overwhelming sensory situations, explained my social difficulties in conversations that felt a bit awkward, and even asked for an extracurricular director's help when I was faced with the particularly daunting task of going on a trip.

Learning about the differences between high school and college social scenes, and then thinking about possible strategies for navigating this new environment, can help Autistic students be as ready as possible for the social side of college.

Asking questions about available accommodations

In college, faculty and staff may not necessarily come to you and ask you what you need. So it's up to the student (and, potentially, their advocates/allies) to make sure they find out and take advantage of what's available, as well as—where relevant—what they are entitled to, on both the legal and institutional levels.

While the details vary from country to country, students will typically obtain an accommodation letter from the appropriate college office and then share it with their professors.

Note that both obtaining this letter and sharing it are the responsibility of the student, which can be a lot to deal with.

On the other hand, there are a variety of ways in which college-level learning can be especially suited to students who learn differently. For example, college professors may have more leeway to be flexible around assignments and deadlines than high school teachers. Things like smaller class sizes (at least in upper-level courses), faculty office hours, and diverse course topics (more on this below) can also encourage and nurture neurodivergent students.

Several respondents mentioned the injustice of participation-based grading, which is common at the college level. One respondent (she/her) explains, "Some of my grades in college and graduate school were influenced by the level of participation. I felt that this was quite ableist since I struggled (and continue to struggle) with selective mutism." One respondent (she/they) says, "I struggle to participate in class and talk in front of others. I wish there were more acceptance and opportunities for written works, and less importance on the oral marks."

A frank discussion regarding concerns with the professor (face to face, in writing, or via assistive technology) and/or the school's office for disability, accommodations, and/or learning differences may result in fairer, more inclusive practices for the Autistic young person—and perhaps for other learners as well.

Accommodations also encompass residential, social, and wellness aspects of college life. Like Lessard (she/her), for whom "sharing a room was something that seemed like it would be too much of an undertaking," and Gallant (she/her), who found that the "difficulty with living in a dorm room made my mental health very low while I was a freshman," many Autistic students who choose to live on campus prefer a single room or a quieter living situation, and should discuss this with the office concerned with residential life during the room-selection process. Some colleges offer hybrid solutions with private bedrooms and shared living rooms. Some respondents mentioned benefiting from social or mental health supports. Others discussed needing scaffolding for executive function, behavioral, and other practical skills. These needs may be addressed by available staff, faculty, and peer programs or groups, but again, each student is responsible for accessing and following through on them.

Taking advantage of opportunities to branch out

No more parents to hover around and tell you what to do? Great! Now what? Cordeiro (they/them) describes feeling very positive about "branching out, learning about what I love, having the chance to step out of my comfort zone" in college. Students attending community college or living at home will also encounter opportunities to get involved in activities outside the classroom.

All institutions of higher learning aim to serve the whole student, and that generally includes providing or hosting non-academic offerings that facilitate learning, connections, activism, health, and personal growth. These may include athletics, clubs, activities, trips, entertainment, affinity groups, and more, along with academic-adjacent gatherings, such as birdwatching, stargazing, and museum outings.

Once again, it's up to the students themselves to participate. Autistic students may find it easier to start with online school-affiliated groups and perhaps make connections there that may blossom into real-life outings. But the nice thing about taking a chance on new activities of this sort is that you already know you share an interest—even if that just means an interest in trying something new!—with other participants.

Building independence in new ways

Taking risks is a big part of growing. Many aspects of transitioning to college life will give Autistic students opportunities to become responsible for themselves in new, exciting, sometimes daunting—or even downright terrifying—ways. From choosing classes and social activities to making their way to the dining hall, completing assignments to proactively accessing any supports they might need, Autistic college students will find themselves faced with exponentially increased chances to manage their own time and energy. They'll also usually be away from home for the first time, which can be hard! For Lessard (she/her), "Adjusting to being away from home was my biggest challenge, and it's still difficult."

Each student will need to develop independence at their own safe, healthy pace. Becoming familiar with the resources available at your college and asking for help may be key aspects of this journey.

Exploring more interesting topics

Choosing a college that offers classes and majors that interest you is a fundamental part of picking the right one. A college course catalog can be thrilling to students previously limited to standard high school class topics. Plus, students can eventually choose a major that aligns with their skills and passions, and build knowledge that will enrich their lives and careers. One respondent (she/they) was looking forward to being more engaged in the classroom once they got to college, "I hope that the topics will generally be a bit more interesting as they are tailored to the field of study I chose."

There are very few other times in life in which people are actively encouraged to learn about such a wide range of fascinating things. Students who are open and curious will be able to explore all sorts of subjects, as well as integrate learning with their interest spikes. Many colleges and universities also offer faculty-supervised, self-directed learning, usually once required courses in a subject have been completed.

Bridge (they/them) loved this aspect of higher education:

I really enjoyed having the freedom to choose what I wanted to learn about (for the most part) and the flexibility of doing things that I wanted to do. I managed to pitch projects to my professors and they let me do them.

149

Preparing for new opportunities and challenges in a college environment can enable Autistic college students to tackle this major transition with effective mindsets, strategies, tools, and resources.

Navigating early independence, No. 2: Choosing an internship, volunteer work, or a job

Whether or not you choose to continue your education after high school, thinking about working, volunteering, apprenticing, interning, or participating in a job-training program may be an important part of early independence. Earning and managing your own money—when possible!—is a big aspect of making your own choices and taking on adult responsibilities. Making sure you find work activities that are meaningful to you, and that take place in a workplace where you matter, where you are seen and heard, is one of the most important steps in life for many people.

Since Autistic people may encounter more barriers in this area, and may advance at their own pace, we cover this topic from several angles—in the context of high school considerations, in Step 5, above; through the transition to independence, here; and in Step 7, from a more comprehensive perspective on advocacy, self-advocacy, and allyship in work environments.

This section sows the seeds of thinking about work-related topics as young people begin to move toward their particular expression of independence. Sections in this book that explore how to create, or help create, a refuge where you can rest and build up spoons, as well as sections on finding and building positive interpersonal connections and environments, may also be helpful.

Young people often try several kinds of job/volunteer/ intern positions before finding one or more that provide a good fit. Some continue to work at a succession of different jobs, while others may feel drawn toward a particular career. Career work is typically more specialized, requires related work experience and/or a degree, and is undertaken for a longer period of time, ideally with opportunities for advancement.

One respondent (NP) describes the resources they think would be useful for Autistic job-seekers, including improved job training and more extensive employment options. Autistic young adults may also want to look into online, vocational rehabilitation, school, or other resources or agencies that can help with resume-writing and looking for work.

The above respondent's insights also point to another issue Autistic young people face: being Autistic often makes it harder to find, get, and keep a job. So this whole process can take longer and require more effort—from people who may already be experiencing overload in other ways. Ernesto (he/him) suggests practicing patience with yourself and/or the Autistic people in your life as you/they attempt to take steps toward working: "Personally, finding jobs can be a tough one and maybe just less pressure around that stuff [would help]."

When looking for opportunities in these areas, some respondents advised making sure participants have the chance to grow. As one respondent (she/her) explains, it may be best to avoid workplaces or programs that steer employees, interns, or volunteers into dead-end occupations, like the one she found herself in, where "there was no encouragement for any of the participants to do things other than clean up trash." On the other hand, if you love a particular activity, or feel you are being of service in a meaningful way, you may not mind doing it for years or decades.

In any case, first steps toward employment don't need to be permanent—it's just good to have a thorough idea of what you are getting into. Here are some things to consider at this stage.

Being aware of how intersectionality can factor into the work world

Multiple discriminations may impact Autistic young people as they pursue shorter-term or career employment. Autistic workers—especially those experiencing intersectional identities, for example, BIPOC, female, multiply disabled, and/or LGBTQIA+—risk financial, interpersonal, cultural, and other discriminations in just about every path of employment, even as their work may provide much-needed income and independence.

Bridge (they/them) describes how this can manifest:

> With a completed Master's degree and an extensive resume, I was only making $10,000 a year doing front-line social service work part time. Despite all my abilities and skills, I went unrecognized and was often discriminated against for being a trans woman, for being fat, for being mixed race, for being disabled, and for being autistic. It was really disheartening.

Pressure to mask at work is another depleting impact of intersectionality. Biologically born female Autistic people, for example, often feel compelled to mask as typically "feminine." One respondent (she/her) explains that

> ...society puts a lot of pressure on women to behave a certain way. Naturally, my voice is more monotone and I am not very expressive. I've learned to exaggerate my facial expressions to the point of being comical. My voice is bubbly and upbeat, intentionally. I find it very exhausting to put on this mask every day. I spend a lot of time trying to make people more comfortable with me.

BIPOC workers may feel pressure to double-mask—that is, also as "white"—in certain workplaces. As Studemire (she/her) points out:

My experiences as a Black disabled woman are not going to be the same as a white disabled woman's. There may be some overlaps, which is what intersection is about. But unfortunately, the way I'm treated while navigating the world...is impacted by both my disabilities and the color of my skin.

Bottom line, intersectional Autistic youth often have to work harder than their NT, white, cisgender, and otherwise-privileged counterparts to get hired, get their job done, interact in "acceptable" ways, stay employed, and so on. Corporations and other institutions are evolving. And young Autistic voices, along with allies and advocates, are playing a large role in that growth. But it's important to be cognizant of the very real effects of intersectionality as you make your way into the world of work.

Thinking about how to handle disclosure and accommodations

Step 7 will have more practical advice and tips for making disclosure decisions and requesting and accessing accommodations, but we wanted to bring these topics up in this section because the years when you are transitioning toward early adulthood are a great time to begin considering where you stand on sharing your neurodivergence, as well as what adaptations or modifications you might need for workplace equity and success.

Employment laws around disability vary by country, but most nations have certain protections that are intended to prevent workplace discrimination based on disability. These laws support people with differences and disabilities in obtaining work, as well as in succeeding on the job. Cordeiro (they/them) found that having a certain legal status was useful: "I am also legally registered as disabled, which allows me to get support."

But many Autistic people feel ambivalent about disclosure,

whether because their neurodivergence feels like a private matter, they fear being underestimated or fired, or a variety of other reasons.

Emily (she/her) expresses this mixed perspective:

> I worked so well from home during the pandemic...but now my employer wants me back in the office more... I know my work quality will suffer because of this, and if I mention my Autism I might be allowed some accommodations, but I almost feel like I shouldn't have to mention something so private to me. I have shown how well I can work from home. I do not get any employment support—I've never felt the need to access this.

When beginning to consider these decisions, there are several central issues to think about, starting with the relevant law, workplace culture (more on this below), and what will feel most empowering to you (or the Autistic young person you are advocating/allying with). To make informed choices around needs, disclosure, and accommodations, it's also vital to think about how you/they will experience various aspects of the work environment, including the work itself.

Understanding the pros and cons of different types of work

Autistic young people seeking employment have at least two vital factors to juggle: unless they are dealing with a company or organization that actively recruits ND employees or practices radically inclusive workplace policies, they need to find a good fit both in terms of the work itself and regarding their neurodivergence. This section discusses the possibilities for the former; the latter is covered in the next section.

There are so many jobs and careers out there, so make sure plenty of research into the vast range of possibilities is a central part of the job-search process. We only learn about various types of work by exploring the options, which are far more diverse than most young people realize, encompassing everything imaginable, from working with animals to assembling rockets, professional jazz musician to non-profit advocacy work! Some pay well, some less so, some require working in an office or other work space, others may be home-based or solely or partly online...the choices are almost infinite.

Before they even start to make decisions about which type of job to aim for, Autistic young people should think about what they are good at, or could learn to be good at, along with credentials they might have that would qualify them for a position. They can also integrate their interests into this process—we spend a lot of time at work and it's better if we like what we are doing!

For those who can't afford to take the time for all that pondering, or for whom hands-on experience is key, trying out various positions may eventually be rewarding. After working at several jobs that didn't feel inclusive or utilize her skills, Chloe (she/her) found a position with the (UK) National Health Service where she feels both content and useful: "I help educate people about Autism and Autistic people. I also come up with ideas on how to make services more inclusive and try to point out where there are problems in the service that need improvements." Jenny, too, explored a wide range of careers before landing on something (writing and editing) that suited her introverted personality and academic/creative skill sets. Similarly, Blackham (she/her) chose a freelance career that suits her skills and needs:

> Looking back, I had enormous problems coping with my job in my twenties working in a huge open-plan office. I was notorious for having "meltdowns" in the workplace. I think in many other companies I would have been disciplined for my behaviour, but I was working as a technical editor of computer programming manuals, and I was far from the only undiagnosed autistic on the payroll. After that, I've always worked from home. As a freelance book

editor, I'm free to choose my own hours. I also only work part time as an associate lecturer and my institution (the Open University) is entirely distance learning at the undergraduate level, so remote working at times of my choosing is the norm. I've basically set my life up to work around my limitations. I'm very blessed.

The point is, different types of work have very different requirements when it comes to time, energy, interaction, personality, physical and mental labor, training, talent, education, knowledge, and so on, as well as widely divergent work environments.

Looking for welcoming environments

Finding genuinely inclusive work environments (and avoiding toxic ones) is of paramount importance for Autistic young adults as they make their way toward their own visions of independence and success. Places that welcome diverse employees tend to look diverse. You may see people of varied ethnicities, genders, and ages, using assistive technology, mobility devices, noise-canceling headphones, and so on.

While a truly welcoming environment will ideally welcome all people in any way necessary—from culture to decor, policies to accommodations, and so on—the details most important to a given person may vary. For one respondent (he/him), for example, a welcoming environment is one in which people (including leadership, human resources, and so on) are very clear about rules, expectations, and work policies. He discovered this only after having "several jobs":

> Some I really liked and was good at, others were very stressful and I couldn't keep the job because I didn't understand what was expected of me and I seemed to constantly not meet the expectations I couldn't figure out. I need detailed instructions and a clear picture of what is expected of me

so I know if I'm doing well. If I can't measure my own progress, it makes me very anxious.

For Cordeiro (they/them), inclusivity entails accepting that we all work at our own pace: "The animal shelter that I work for allows me to take things at a very slow pace, which is always helpful."

Forrester (any/varies) appreciates co-workers who lighten the load by being encouraging and accepting. They explain, "It's been a little difficult, but I mostly enjoy my job and have supportive co-workers. I had to buy headphones to tune out office noise and conversations."

Welcoming workplaces involve people, cultures, policies, and sensory and built environments, but they also involve more subtle things. Is someone willing to unpack that unspoken social code for you so that you have the information you need to make informed decisions—and at least know the assumptions others are acting under? Will you be accepted and welcome if you present, act, or choose differently from the status quo? Or is the status quo already heterogeneous? Given your identities, personality, skills, values, needs, and goals, will you feel as if you belong in this space?

Navigating early independence, No.3: Getting a driver's license/ figuring out transportation

The freedom to get where you want or need to go is a fundamental aspect of adulthood. For this reason, learning to drive and getting a driver's license can be a meaningful and important step. But it's not something that everyone wants— and it's not achievable for everybody, either. Non-driving or car-less Autistic youth have options as well. Many areas have extensive public transportation, and most have at least some resources for people who need to get around but do not drive or own a car, including programs for people with disabilities. Ride-sharing services can be very helpful for those who can afford them. Investigating the possibilities in your area may be a crucial step toward independence.

Driving can be incredibly overwhelming. The whole process—learning to drive, getting one's license, keeping current on licensing, registration, and vehicle upkeep, and the act of driving itself—requires a vast range of skills, including multitasking, coordination, executive function, money management, proprioception, and social interaction. These requirements can pose challenges for some Autistic people. Thus, Autistic youth drive at a proportionately lower rate than their NT peers. Millennials and Gen Z are also less likely to drive than prior generations for a variety of reasons, including better alternative transportation options and the environmental costs of driving.

At the same time, driving can be an integral element of independence, especially where there is limited public transportation. So driving is really a right, albeit one that must be earned by gaining knowledge and passing tests. Supports are available, too. Local vocational rehabilitation departments (or similar), for example, likely run programs for Autistic people who want to learn to drive. And by the way, statistics show that Autistic youth are safer drivers than NT young people (Curry, 2021)!

In the course of figuring out how to remove any possible obstacles from the learning process, advocates, self-advocates, and allies should consider several factors. As a few respondents mentioned, many new drivers prefer to learn on a stick shift, rather than a manual transmission. Applying study skills learned in other subjects can be helpful when preparing for the written test. For Marsh (they/them), "The written test was annoying and crummy, but I was motivated and put all my energy into studying and did fine." It's also generally helpful to hold early driving practice in a safe, non-overwhelming place, such as an empty parking lot or cemetery. For one respondent (she/her), "It helped that I learned to drive on a farm with no traffic or signs, focusing initially on simply handling the vehicle." Similarly, reducing sensory overload inside the car—avoiding air fresheners, not talking unless necessary, keeping the stereo off—can promote better focus for new Autistic drivers.

Finding an instructor who is comfortable and adept at teaching neurodivergent students is also key. In Bridge's (they/them) words, "I will try and learn to drive at some point in my life, but I'll need someone who's sensitive to my needs." It may be necessary to collaborate with the instructor or others involved to find ways to facilitate the Autistic person's learning (such as visual or auditory inputs, or physical gestures, as one respondent suggests below). But it's important not to give up! You might have to try more than once before you pass the driving test. Anonymous (NP) explains:

> It took me three times to pass my test. I really struggled, as I get my lefts and rights muddled, so found it hard to follow verbal instructions. Hand gestures from my driving instructor and examiner helped though.

Autistic young adults may learn to drive in their own time. Forrester (any/varies), who didn't get their license until they were 23, "was terrified of driving, mostly because my mom taught me to drive and she had driving anxiety. Once I got my license, I found driving easy." Abramowski (she/her) says, "I wasn't in a hurry to drive at first, so I waited a little longer. Once I started, I learned it wasn't too much of a challenge for me! I can't imagine not driving now!" Jenny didn't drive until her late 30s!

Considering the potential benefits, such as increased independence
Weighing the pros and cons of learning to drive can help each person decide whether it's worth pursuing. As our respondents

have shared, getting a driver's license can be hard work. But it can also give young adults much-needed freedom, as well as access to employment, socializing, and other opportunities they would otherwise be unable to take advantage of.

Lucy (she/her) found that the whole ordeal was worth it in the end because it enabled her to get where she wanted to go on her own:

> Driving is like the final act, for me. I failed my written test for my learner's license three times and felt so dumb. And now, almost 35 (!), thanks to a change in how the learner's license is obtained, I was able to get it. I love the idea of going anywhere I want at any time, and my city's public transport isn't that great, especially where I live, so you need reliable (and sometimes reluctant) transport or to do it yourself.

For some respondents, driving is an unmitigated good. Kimble (she/her) says, "I love driving!" Like one anonymous respondent (she/her) and Nora (she/her), Kimble finds driving relatively easy and fun. Birch (she/her), too, finds driving itself easy, but struggles with overwhelm from "the sensory fracas around me, such as lights and car horns." For others, a driver's license is something they aspire to but have yet to obtain.

Being able to drive can mitigate some of the barriers to success Autistic young adults may face. It can open doors, build a sense of accomplishment and self-respect, and elicit respect from others. Thus, many Autistic youth consider driving a valuable skill that may be worth whatever efforts are required to get a license. Learning about and utilizing public or other transportation options can provide many of the same benefits.

Weighing the potential negatives, such as anxiety

For many of us, the prospect of driving creates major anxiety or seems difficult or even impossible based on our physical, sensory, and other differences. Other young Autistic people opt out of driving or choose to delay learning to drive until later in life for any number of reasons, including financial ones.

The negatives around getting a driver's license can be daunting. One respondent (she/her) is nervous, but nonetheless intends to proceed:

> I have obtained my learner's permit, but I am very anxious about driving. I haven't practiced much, but there is a lot to remember and a lot to focus on. You also have to stay calm. I'm very scared because there's a lot that can go wrong.

Similarly, one respondent (she/her) hopes to learn but feels constrained by a variety of obstacles, from anxiety to a feeling that even thinking about driving is a big energy drain.

Having gone through the process, Vu (he/him) details the ups and downs of his experience as ultimately worthwhile:

> For me, learning to drive was a bit difficult as I get scared of doing things wrong, and having the risk of crashing the car or making illegal moves continued to loom over my head. Plus, I sometimes had aggressive driving instructors who would chide me loudly, which would scare me even more. While I managed to get my driver's license and learned how to self-cope and adapt to my environment in the end, I could definitely say that learning to drive was a bit frightening, although I ended up being grateful for now knowing how to take myself and others around in the long run.

Other Autistic youth are choosing not to drive, possibly ever. Corrado (she/her) feels she is "too distracted," and another (anonymous) respondent is "afraid of getting into a crash." One respondent (she/her) cites both anxiety and difficulty focusing as reasons not to drive, while Ierubino (he/him) worries it could be "confusing." And Cordeiro (they/them) says,

"Driving is nearly impossible. I notice too many visual details and get overwhelmed. I also am dyspraxic, which makes it harder to coordinate movement." All those details were one of the main reasons Jenny avoided driving for so long, but she has managed to learn to focus on the important visuals and sounds over time.

Since driving can present more challenges for Autistic people, learning to drive can also be more expensive, as Chloe (she/her) notes: "It's an area where Autistic people are let down, and I find it unfair." Maclean (NP) mentions both their "fear of driving" and the cost of driving to college as obstacles.

Autistic young people are also understandably put off by the potential harms caused by other drivers. Birch (she/her) is concerned about "the fact that I have no control over what the other cars are doing," while one respondent (she/they) struggles with "predicting other drivers' reactions." Topographical agnosia can also be an issue (as it is for Jenny): one respondent (she/they) notes, "I find it really hard to remember the way, even to places I am quite familiar with."

Together, these myriad negative factors may deter some Autistic youth from driving, while others will choose to master this potentially useful skill in their own ways, at their own pace. Public transportation and other options for getting around, such as ride-sharing or mobility services for people with disabilities, can be incredibly useful for those who cannot or choose not to drive. And perhaps self-driving technology will continue to advance and become more accessible to the general population. What a game-changer that would be for so many disabled people!

Navigating early independence, No. 4: Living independently

Independent living looks different for everybody, whether it means remaining with family but with more independence as appropriate over time, living on one's own as a single person, cohabitating with a partner, having a roommate or several, or living in a communal or group household. If they want or hope to do so, there are many things that can help Autistic young people gain independence in their living situation and have their own space.

Many of our respondents reported satisfaction and ease with independent living. Baik (she/her), for example, says, "I live on my own. I never needed 'help' because I'm fiercely independent and highly capable and self-sufficient. It came naturally to me." One respondent (she/her), who's been living "alone for more than ten years," and Harrington (she/her), who is "happily married," have few difficulties with living independently.

Others have used shorter or trial periods of independence to gain essential living skills. Nora (she/her), for example, says, "I got the opportunity to live apart from my parents for three months over the summer, and I used that time to figure out how that all works, and I don't really need any special accommodations." Still others dream of ideal future living conditions that would suit them perfectly, such as one respondent's (she/her) vision of "a quiet area and maybe a small house to myself."

While these positive experiences reflect the fact that many Autistic people are easily able to live on their own, the shift to this aspect of greater independence can be more—sometimes much more—challenging for some. Fortunately, there are plenty of ways for Autistic people to support themselves, or to be supported, in the journey toward living independently. We outline some of the most important ones below.

Remembering independence is often a gradual process

Whether an Autistic young person wants to be entirely responsible for their own living space or simply wants to evolve toward other elements of personal freedom while living in a more supportive environment (such as a family or group home), they must—and will—do so at their own pace.

We heard from some people who plan to live at home, in some instances for the foreseeable future. Tino (he/him) says, "I am not able to live alone because of my body issues." Abramowski (she/her) isn't sure when, or if, she will ever move out: "I continue to live at home with my mom. I have no intention of leaving in the near future. That's a bridge I'll cross when I get to it."

Unfortunately, resources and programs for Autistic youth can be in short supply after high school, which can further delay the process of becoming independent. Day (e/em/eir) bemoans the lack of support experienced by many young adult and adult Autistic people. E explains that unless they have been identified as having high support needs and are thus eligible for group or supportive housing and wraparound services, Autistic adults may have a hard time accessing assistance with taking care of themselves, experienced autism-friendly therapists, help with housing needs, and more.

As one respondent (NP) notes, we need to take advantage of (or develop, where unavailable) programs that can help Autistic young adults learn to live on their own and gain life skills. Of course, "full independence" may mean different things for different people at different times. What most Autistic young people do share, however, is the desire to be respected—and respectfully supported or scaffolded, where necessary and appropriate—when it comes to making their own choices, in their own time, about their lives and living spaces. This holds true for those taking the first steps toward independent living, as it does for those who already successfully live on their own.

Knowing the differences between supportive and unsupportive advocacy efforts

Simply put, supportive advocacy efforts presume competence, affirm the integrity and autonomy of Autistic young adults, and honor their preferences, hopes, goals, and dreams. Unsupportive advocacy efforts ignore Autistic young people's wants, experiences, and perspectives, infantilize or marginalize them, deny their rights as human beings, and undermine their efforts toward autonomy.

How can we distinguish between these two types of advocacy in the journey toward self-determination? Both our first book and this one promote principles that should underlie any advocacy efforts, and, if adhered to, prevent advocacy that belittles and harms Autistic people. But since the path toward independence can often be more complicated and prolonged than it usually is for NTs, it's important to be especially mindful around supporting the entire process. Our respondents shared a variety of insights in this area.

Teaching practical skills is one positive way to nurture self-sufficiency. One respondent (she/her) notes that her mother taught her how to cook some recipes, which she found very helpful. Other areas of expertise that might be helpful to young Autistic people could include cleaning, yardwork, hygiene, healthy eating, physical fitness, laundry, bill-paying, money management, sewing, carpentry, car repair, and so on.

And never underestimate the value of plain old unconditional support—family, professional, community. Kimble (she/her) says the one thing that will matter most for living on her own will be "support from my family," while Emily (she/her) relies on "regular check-ins and ongoing support from my family and healthcare practitioners." Cordeiro (they/them) says, "If I were to live alone, I would love a strong sense of community support."

Expressing faith in people's capabilities is part of genuinely supportive advocacy efforts. Vaughan (she/her) explains, "I find it challenging knowing that once I'm out of high school, I feel like I have a higher chance of failure. Reassurance would help." So would acknowledging the difficulties faced by Autistic people in this endeavor. Springfield (he/him) says:

Being on my own/independent and having the weight of that responsibility as well as the idea that sometimes I won't have someone supporting me, but having people who understand what I'm going through in moments of vulnerability, is what will drive me.

Therapists and other professionals who are Autistic and/or autism-aware and neuro-affirming can also provide real help as Autistic young people expand their horizons. Indeed, having people around you—whether professionals, family, friends, or partners—who unconditionally care about, encourage, and believe in you can make all the difference in this journey. This holds true for Autistic young people whatever their support needs, as Benhamou (NP) points out, "I have people who take care of me and help me have a balance, which allows me a certain independence."

Making a set of rules

What factors might you be missing in your exploration of independent living options? What tasks or necessary activities might you forget or avoid if living somewhat or entirely independently? How exactly does someone learn to live on their own, especially if they may think and learn differently from the NT norm? What's the best way to find and procure a place to live? And how does one make sure they are covering all the bases once established in a home? Marsh (they/them) suggests scaffolding the process of figuring these things out and then following through on them by developing rules for yourself or with an advocate/ally:

> I think making a set of rules would have been helpful. Again, this needs to be driven by the autistic person. How do they want to go about living? Where do they need help? Where and when do they want to be left to their own devices? It's a lot to think about and it's the kind of thing that is best planned for, lived, and then replanned as needed.

Making lists of important things to keep in mind or do can be a hugely helpful tool at all stages of the independent-living process, from beginning to think about your ideal housing context to optimizing a living situation you're already in. For example, a list of guidelines for practical necessities, such as bill-paying and cleaning, can be really useful when you are moving into, or living in, your own or a shared space. You might use a digital or paper calendar with monthly tasks, such as bill-paying, weekly tasks, like grocery shopping or doing laundry, and daily chores, including showering and brushing your teeth. Your list might include rules for self-regulation (sleep schedule, eating habits, screen consumption) or executive function (for example, the various steps and elements involved in making a budget and sticking to it, or the multiple obligations involved in health-care and insurance). Generating a set of rules can also help you think about what's most important to you, and how to prioritize those things. It's good to include activities or events you look forward to, in addition to necessary tasks!

People with experience in independent living can provide useful information to ensure your list of rules is comprehensive, while you—or the Autistic person you are helping out in this area—can ensure it's in line with your/their values, goals, dreams, needs, and skills. Perhaps proximity to certain amenities or resources really matters to you, or you want to live in a building with no fluorescent lighting. Maybe you prefer a very quiet environment or want to live in an urban setting. Stuff like that can be part of your rules/list. One respondent (she/they) says, "For me it is important that there are activities nearby that I can do, and I like to have them scheduled so that I can actually stick to it and develop a routine."

For advocates and allies, any such rules should intentionally, explicitly be created or co-created by the Autistic person with whom you are advocating/allying. Advocates, allies, and self-advocates alike should bear in mind that these rules will need to be regularly updated as skills, needs, finances, and other aspects relevant to independent living evolve.

Considering living with a partner or roommate

There's a lot of mental and physical labor involved in keeping a household afloat. Living with a friend, roommate, or partner can supply built-in social interaction, lighten the housekeeping/financial load, and more. One respondent (she/her) points out some of the advantages:

> I feel that living with friends, roommates, or a partner would be better than independent living because I could split the chores, enjoy their company, and would be less able to isolate myself in times of need, all while still living mostly independently.

Having an Autistic housemate makes sense for many Autistic youth for the many reasons detailed in other sections. Forrester (any/varies) says, "I am living on my own and am very happy for it. One of my roommates is autistic." One respondent (NP) dreams of a largely Autistic, mutually helpful household, with some governmental assistance to help keep certain things on track:

> I want to live by myself with my boyfriend and best friend and he has autism too...and we are going to live in a flat and we will do stuff for each other like...I help him with going to the bathroom, and he helps me change, and we get a needs assessment by the government; and they send someone to help us cook and go shopping and get to the doctor, and make sure we brush our teeth and shower and help us clean.

In addition, a roommate can feel like a protective presence for some—like one respondent (she/they), who finds living alone anxiety-provoking explains:

> I wish to live independently, but not completely alone. Being home alone gives me a lot of anxiety, especially at

night, so I like to have a trusted person nearby that I can reach out to. Currently I do not live alone, and struggle with loud noises and having lots of people around, so I think having a soundproof room of my own would be beneficial.

Preferences for levels of noise, interaction, cleanliness, and so on are something to explore and agree on from the outset. If these key things are taken into consideration, the right roommate(s) or partner can ease many of the challenges associated with independent living.

Learning about resources for independent living and money management

Autonomy, including financial autonomy, requires a host of skills. These skills may not be obvious to Autistic people, or they may be hard to master solo or with their current capacities. For example, many young people transitioning to early independence are uninformed about health insurance and healthcare. In countries without a national health insurance program, such as the United States, this can be a huge problem. Young U.S. residents who do not receive disability payments—which are automatically linked with the Medicaid health insurance program—may find themselves responsible for obtaining health insurance. And young people everywhere may become partly or fully responsible for making sure they make and keep the appropriate medical appointments, including wellness visits, and stay consistent with any necessary medications.

How can we get and stay on top of all these new responsibilities? In Moody's (she/her) words, "More independent living resources and money management resources would really help me if I eventually live on my own." One respondent (he/him) outlines his concerns about the many responsibilities that young adults and adults may need to deal with when living on their own:

Handling money and bills was difficult, as well as being responsible for cleaning and doing household chores, making my own appointments, doing grocery shopping, remembering to eat, and having to cook my own meals. I also struggled to remember hygiene tasks on a decent schedule without someone reminding me. I wish there was some kind of manual of step-by-step instructions on everything adults have to know how to do to live independently.

Finding and utilizing governmental, local, and non-profit agencies and resources, including online ones, can be vital to success in these multiple obligations, whether via guidance, assistance, tools, education, or oversight. But it's also important to seek out programs, trainings, professionals, advocates, or allies that can help you (or the Autistic people you care about) build internal resources and life/money skills.

Financial literacy programs benefit people of all neurologies. And learning about building credit, monitoring accounts online (or balancing a checkbook), budgeting, saving, and planning is crucial for any young adult. But these are even more vital for Autistic youth setting out on their unique path toward adulthood.

Vu (he/him) explains:

I think it would help to know how to pay taxes, how to pay bills, and how to do some basic house maintenance. These are skills I still don't have that I don't understand or know how to manage. Is there a school or class to learn all of this? These are essential skills to have that don't seem to be taught often in schools and that sometimes feel as if people are naturally expected to pick up on the spot.

Researching whether your local vocational rehabilitation department or other local organizations offer money-management education geared toward Autistic youth and adults, and then actively participating, will definitely pay off in the long run.

As regards independent living in general, every Autistic young adult will have both unique personal strengths and resources and their own particular resource needs. Ierubino (he/him) suggests some possible areas where he personally excels—and some where he expects to rely on more help:

> First off, I would need help with budgeting my money. Second, I am good with my laundry and grocery shopping. But I'm really not good at cooking meals. I could use support with easy meals. And finally, as long as I have scheduled things to do, I can be much more independent. Without a schedule, I tend to become disorganized.

Whether you do so with someone else, with the help of a program or agency, or on your own, developing a daily, weekly, or monthly schedule can be helpful in much the same way as a set of rules (see above), bringing clarity around meeting expectations and accomplishing the independent-living tasks that need to be addressed, such as bill-paying, hygiene, wellness, and home maintenance.

Becoming informed about what's available for Autistic young adults seeking financial know-how and increased independence, and then participating in the appropriate assistance or program(s), can help with living on one's own. A money-savvy trusted adult (whether that's a family member or banking professional) might be another source of good advice. With their own combination of personal initiative and reliance on available resources, Autistic young adults can improve their money-management skills and build their freedom.

Developing strategies for finding affordable and manageable housing

There are two very different main aspects to strategic, sensible, informed decision-making when it comes to housing:

the financial side and the practical side. First, what can you afford, housing wise, and how will you continue to afford it? Second, how much housing-related responsibility can you manage, and how can you ensure that you are able to meet those responsibilities—or have the help you need to do so— over the longer term? Asking these questions is a crucial part of independent living.

Some resources intended for various subsets of the general population, such as first-time home buyer programs, or low-income (or, in the U.S., Section 8) housing vouchers, may also be useful to Autistic people seeking housing. Housing programs for people with disabilities vary by region, but may provide financial, practical, and other assistance with independent living needs, and make supportive housing available, where appropriate. Step 5 references several guides from ASAN that may help in this area.

Corrado (she/her) says that "having family support, and affordable housing of my choosing, not a housing project, rather, a home in a regular neighbourhood," would enable her to live on her own. Lucy (she/her) shares Corrado's hopes, with some reservations: "I would love to live on my own and hope I do have my own place in the future, but housing is expensive and relies too much on house-sharing."

After a long and grueling advocacy battle, Chloe (she/her) finally received funding and resources for:

> ...the support I need in the community to help me with my day-to-day life to help keep me more stable. Having support workers in five times a week who help me with anything I need support with has changed my life. I'm so much happier and I'm finding living on my own so much easier... I wouldn't be able to function or live alone if it wasn't for this support I get now.

Chloe's experience with "the lack of services for Autistic people" has led her to activism: "I'm trying to fight for the services to support *all* Autistic people" (more on activism in Stage Four of this guide, a free online resource). Others may have fewer support needs as they transition to independent living. For Maclean (NP), for example, living on their own is simply "a matter of finding the right and best place for me." The key is developing an awareness of one's own capacities and needs.

Finding affordable and manageable housing is yet another aspect of early independence that can go much more smoothly when the person seeking housing has plenty of information throughout the process.

Conclusion: Gaining knowledge, tools, and clarity to achieve early independence

Step 6 is our longest chapter. The extensive aspects of navigating early independence pose some of the most daunting challenges and exciting opportunities in the lives of Autistic young people. #ActuallyAutistic experiences and perspectives can provide immeasurable aid in this process.

As one respondent (he/him) explains, many Autistic young adults will be more likely to succeed in meeting their own independence goals if they can access supportive, autism-friendly, inclusive help with the various factors involved. He recommends an "adulting class that teaches interview skills, resume-writing, budgeting and building credit, the process of renting/buying houses, and the process of buying a car."

Whether or not they have access to an actual "adulting class," we hope this chapter enables Autistic young adults and those who care about them to create a proactive, personalized vision of early independence. Integrating the necessary practical skills and available resources, along with personal strengths, needs, and dreams, will increase the likelihood of realizing that vision.

SUMMARY GUIDANCE:
#ActuallyAutistic practical tips
for early independence

- Know that you have choices—and that more knowledge will improve the odds of making good choices.
- Be aware that attending a higher education institution (college, vocational school, or community college) may look different in terms of timelines, supports, accommodations, and other things for different people.
- Be patient with both yourself and/or the Autistic person/people in your life throughout the sometimes lengthy process of figuring out employment. Learning about work and what might be a good fit, building a resume and work skills, trying different jobs out, participating in a job-training program, obtaining a career-oriented position, volunteering, interning, and apprenticing are all useful, meaningful activities.
- Weigh the unique pros and cons of driving for you and/or the Autistic person/people in your life.
- Know that developing a set of tailored rules can help people make choices about how they want to live. Another set of rules can enable them to live successfully in their own version of independence.
- Consider using this chapter to map out relevant aspects of early independence, incorporating personal strengths, needs, and dreams as well as practical considerations.

REFLECTION QUESTIONS

? What are your hopes, dreams, and priorities for early independence and how can you take steps now to ensure you are moving toward them? (What are the hopes, dreams, and priorities of the Autistic person/people in your life and how can you support them in moving toward them?) What public, local, non-profit, online, professional, or interpersonal resources might help in this process?

? What seems most daunting about the post-high school stage and what can you (or the Autistic people in your life) do to address it?

? What do you (or the Autistic people in your life) need to do to prepare for the very next step—even if it's a small step—in your (their) independence journey?

? In what ways does intersectionality impact your process of early independence (or that of the Autistic people you care about), including potentially pursuing higher education, working, driving, and independent living?

? How can you (or the Autistic person you care about) best access transportation—by learning to drive? Mastering public transport? Some other way?

? What are some important self-care habits that might truly support healthy transitions to young adulthood for Autistic people?

? How can you (or the Autistic person/people you care about) begin to earn money, if appropriate/ necessary? How can you (or the Autistic person/ people you care about) learn about and practice good financial habits?

? What help might you (or the Autistic people in your life) need to live independently? What skills do you (they) bring to the process?

Advocating for More Inclusive Workplaces and Communities

Flourishing in society as a young adult/adult might include finding a meaningful job to achieve personal or career goals or support your financial needs. And it will likely involve being active in your community in a variety of ways. Advocating for inclusive workplaces and community spaces is essential to ensuring more people have the chance to live, work, and participate in activities according to their own choices, needs, and dreams. A solid understanding of inclusion (and the willingness to implement it in workplaces and communities) makes it easier for people to achieve independence and lead self-determined lives. Steps 7 and 8 offer advice for building more inclusive workplaces and public spaces that help people become more comfortable and capable working and living in their communities, thereby creating more opportunities for independence and interaction, along with immeasurable other life enhancements.

Step 7

Practice Autism-Friendly Workplace and Career Advocacy

Workplace culture was a new minefield to navigate. Especially with things like higher executive function demands and office politics.

—SARA (SHE/HER)

As educational supports disappear on graduation, Autistic young adults are often left to figure out the work transition on their own. Whereas they might have had an IEP, 504, or other education plan in place during school that followed them from teacher to teacher, after graduation they need to make new decisions about what, when, and how to disclose their needs. This is a whole new world where a self-advocacy plan (one that is either collaborative or managed privately) becomes critical. This section covers how to begin the process of finding a good job/career fit, preparing for interviews, how to handle disclosure, and self-advocating in the workplace.

It's written with the understanding that it can take a while to find, obtain, and retain work, and that changing jobs is a fact of life for many people. These tips will help improve the process and make good outcomes more likely for Autistic and NT employers, potential employees, and employees alike.

Practicing autism-friendly workplace and career advocacy, No. 1: Research the best types of employment to find the right field

Why is this needed?

Researching the best employment fit, including employment field, work environment, and schedule options will help you transition into a more predictable and pleasant career/work experience. Some respondents conducted this search on their own, while others used the support of family, friends, or vocational rehabilitation services (or the local equivalent). Finding work that is interesting, meaningful, and suited to one's skills is obviously important, but so is finding a healthy schedule, whether full or part time, and remote or on-site. Compensation is also a concern. Research into the best employment fit requires introspection and self-evaluation, which will be a helpful foundation for the self-advocacy that may be necessary in a new work environment.

Sarah L. (she/her) offers these insights:

> My most important piece of advice would be to do worksite visits of careers you are interested in. Many people will advise you to follow your passions, but it is more important to choose a career that can be modified to fit your specific needs. Pay is also important. If you prefer to live alone, that will be more expensive, so you need to plan for that.

Finding the right fit for particular interests, accommodation needs, and comfort levels

Sometimes people have a sensible grasp of what they are good at or interested in, but other factors (whether finances, concern with prestige, family pressures, abuse, practical issues, curiosity, etc.) push them away from what they are truly passionate about. Shekhar (she/her) says that she joined a software firm out of "social pressure": "I had to look successful. And I had no other ideas for how I'd do that." This position went well for her, and she was promoted, but the promotion required her to learn some specific skills she wasn't very interested in. She shares how she eventually moved out of this position into one that she was more passionate about—teaching:

> I didn't want to waste more time studying something I didn't like. So my mentor pushed me to reflect and figure out what I really wanted to do with my life... I got posted to another department where I managed 300 people and big-ticket projects worth millions of rupees. But I wasn't satisfied... Since my high school, I had been a volunteer teacher. So when I asked my mother one day what really lit me up, she said teaching.

Several others talked about the importance of meaningful work and how they found it. One respondent (she/her) feels "lucky to have a job as a researcher focusing on my special interest. It has not been difficult to find employment in academia." Vu (he/him) says:

> I've luckily managed to find a couple of jobs that I'm proud to have through the workplace and school connections I've had—something I've learned to leverage when dealing with this chaotic job market. While the jobs I got weren't exactly what I expected, they were pretty meaningful experiences to have and have surprisingly helped shape my career interests and goals.

In the current geopolitical climate, many worry that we can't always rely on inclusivity and protected accommodations, but must also take on much of the burden of figuring out where and how we can best function work wise. Leaving aside for the moment how unjust this is (we discuss political advocacy in depth in Step 10 of Stage Four, found online) it's always good to be as self-aware as possible about an activity you may spend the bulk of your time engaged in. Regarding the United States, Sarah L. (she/her) says:

> Although we still have the ADA [Americans with Disabilities Act] to protect us, it is becoming harder and harder to get bosses and co-workers on board with providing work accommodations. It's best to think ahead and choose a career and company that will require the fewest accommodations. For example, if you prefer interacting with one person at a time rather than a group, then choose tutoring instead of teaching. If you know that fluorescent lights give you headaches, then choose a career that takes place in natural lighting. If you know you need a lot of structure, then think twice about freelancing. If you're sensitive to loud noises, avoid retail establishments that play music constantly. Good luck!

Handling scheduling/setting details in a proactive way

Finding work schedules and settings that are comfortable is also a consideration. Some people enjoy the flexibility of virtual rather than in-person meetings. Corrado (she/her) says, "I find that Zoom is easier because I can control the sensory and setting." Virtual meetings allow for different kinds of flexibility and control, offering a variety of ways for people to process information and communicate with others. Transcriptions, recordings, audio controls, camera settings, and a customized workspace are all possible with this medium.

The potential for travel is another work schedule consideration. Sankar (he/him) explains that travel heightens his anxiety and can limit the opportunities Autistic people have:

> Feeling out of control in the very last place you want to lose

it makes the work of travel very hard. This is the reason we try to stay in one place. This is lost autistic opportunity. Lost opportunity gets autistics fearful of lowering their place in the world. The tally of lost opportunities is high. The work autistics put into getting to places is too high. To travel is to be visible. Being visible is to reach our authentic autistic selves.

Anxiety can cause issues in any environment, whether travel is required or not. One respondent (she/her) explains how debilitating her anxiety could be, "I would get very anxious before every shift and feel nauseous for the first three months."

Getting support for the process

Our contributors suggested that external support systems can help people both in the research phase of finding employment and in navigating initial employment decisions to determine whether or not something is a good fit. Harrington (she/her) says, "In terms of support, I turn to my therapist, family, and other places outside the office."

Other people suggested job coaching. Tino (he/him) says he's able to be "rather independent" in two different jobs with the help of a job coach. Similarly, Balfour (she/her) notes that "executive function coaching has been really helpful." Some people may need intensive job coaching and support, while others may only need encouragement and to know they have a place to rest and regroup if things don't work out as they'd hoped.

Many workplaces have a human resources department or office for DEI (diversity, equity, and inclusion). These may offer mentoring programs, employee handbooks, and other resources for understanding work policies and culture, connecting with co-workers, and so on. As with high school and college settings, finding someone who has your back—whether that's a mentor, a fellow Autistic person, a co-worker friend, or some other type of ally—can be really helpful in any workplace.

Balancing the financial and energy hurdles of work *and* school

It can also be difficult to manage new financial hurdles, espe-cially during a transition into part- or full-time employment. If you're working while still in school, these issues can intensify.

Day (e/em/eir) explains e gave up on higher education and training for new careers:

> I tried three times and dropped out each time. I have wanted it so badly, and there are careers I would love to have and could actually do, but can't because I can't get through higher education. One of the biggest hurdles...is the fact that I do not have enough energy to cope with the stress of working as well as going to school, but can't get the funding necessary to cover both my schooling and my regular bills (rent, food, etc.). I have no choice but to work on top of schooling, but I can't handle it.

Working while taking classes can be difficult, so it's important to consider a variety of different ways this can be managed. This might mean taking one class at a time while living at home and working part or full time. Some people may be able to find opportunities to work seasonally while attending classes during non-work periods.

This will naturally go more smoothly with some support from family, friends, partners, professionals, and others, who can offer emotional support, provide a stable home, and help with meals, transportation, money- and time-management, and so on. In fact, these kinds of support can ease the transi-tion from school to work not just for people simultaneously exploring higher education and work, but for anyone experi-encing anxiety or obstacles in the job-search process.

Practicing autism-friendly workplace and career advocacy, No. 2: Prepare for the challenges of interviews

Why is this needed?

First impressions can be lasting, which is sometimes bad news for Autistic people entering job interviews. Interviews put tremendous pressure on Autistic people to mask and figure out how to best showcase their talents and job skills rather than their social differences. Our contributors discussed the difficulties of interviewing, but also shared ideas for inclusive interview practices that help alleviate these barriers.

Masking pressures

Some contributors said they didn't have any issues retaining a job once they'd been able to show off skills or competency in a particular area for a while, but landing the job was tricky. Baik (she/her) says, "I've never had to worry about keeping a job, it's just harder to go through the application process." One respondent (NP) says they "can't talk to people good in interviews" and so they plan to get help from an employment service for disabled people. Ierubino (he/him) says he has been applying for jobs for about a year and has had a few interviews, but never been offered a job: "It is hard to wait to see if you will get a response from the jobs you apply for."

It can be overwhelming to attempt to interact as your best self with a potential employer while trying to remember what you want to share about yourself and your interest in a job. Practicing interview skills with a trusted person can help you emphasize what you bring to the table when you are interviewing for a job or other position (volunteer, etc.). When your job-related credentials, enthusiasm, skills, and abilities are at the forefront, your focus—and hopefully, that of the interviewer—can remain on your strengths, rather than on neuro-normalized concerns, such as whether or not you are successfully masking (or feeling pressure to mask, or trying unsuccessfully to mask) to appear NT.

It's helpful to come to an interview with a plan to demonstrate your skill or experience in a way that is most comfortable for the setting. If it's difficult to articulate in words what you've done and what you're capable of, especially with impromptu questions, then you can come with a portfolio of work, a written summary, or prepared answers you might expect to be asked.

Disclosure of a diagnosis in an interview will also have to be considered (more on this later) if it might help put someone at ease or improve understanding of communication and work preferences. Of course, it's always best when inclusive workplaces and hiring practices are a part of an organization's core mission, as Ciampi (she/her) discusses below regarding Ultranauts, where she is credited for developing an innovative universal design approach for inclusion.

Implementing more equitable recruiting

While these tips for preparing for interviews can be very useful, it's also really important to further workplace policies and processes that welcome a range of potential employees and enable them to shine. Ciampi (she/her) understands that "everybody has some degree of anxiety going into an interview process or recruitment process." She explains how her organization tries to make this as comfortable and straightforward as possible for applicants:

> At Ultranauts, we have a review document that explains what to expect about our process. This way there is no hidden agenda or feeling like you have to sell yourself. Nobody wants to be made to feel they have to play a game to get employment. I try to put myself in the candidate's shoes. I would feel uncomfortable if I didn't know what came next, or if the employer would get back to me, or if I'll just get a form letter response every time... I think what's

best for everybody is to take out the games that naturally come with the hiring process as much as possible and make it more objective.

One example of how they make the interview process more inclusive is by implementing virtual interviews with the option to be off camera. This approach reduces visual stimuli and implicit bias based on visuals, emphasizing skill set and experience instead. Ciampi's experience and insights both remind Autistic people of the many aspects of themselves that may be being evaluated—often unbeknown to them—and suggest ways we can do better in interviews so that all people have a chance to put their best self forward:

> In an interview, you're being judged on what you wear, how you walk, and how you sit. These are all things that autistic people sometimes struggle with, perhaps because of their ligament structure, because of the way they choose not to conform to current hair style or fashion trends. It's important to remove all those what-we-see obstacles, and offer the choice that if someone wants to show their image or be on video, they can.

Ciampi adds that the benefits of a flexible interview policy also reach members of other identities, including the LGBTQIA+ communities, such as transgender individuals:

> If they don't have to go on visuals, they're not going to be subjected to people's preconceived ideas, bias, and other-ing. They're going to be hired for what they share and what they bring, not because of someone's prejudice or thoughts about their way of life.

Ciampi goes on to explain that virtual interviews are also more accessible to people with mobility challenges:

In this day and age, there's really no reason to have initial interviews in-person, unless you want to, and that's awesome because it accommodates a lot of people with physical disabilities who have difficulties driving and getting somewhere. By the time they get there, all their spoons are lost because they're exhausted from chronic pain, or they're exhausted from cognitive functioning, or they have dyslexia or dyspraxia—they're trying to figure out what direction to go: "Do I go right? Do I go left?" and so on.

Ciampi also explains that inclusive practices must be built into every level of the organization, not just the HR team: "We need to be ambassadors, to represent the company in a way that really stands true with the organization's mission and the dignity of all human beings." She suggests that organizations should make it their mission to help underrepresented groups, "such as people who are members of a certain race who have been historically oppressed and historically not given equal opportunity."

Finding or helping to create a workspace that truly values DEI initiatives and inclusive hiring practices is a wonderful option. Even if employees in a given organization aren't professionally trained in how to create an inclusive workspace, finding (or becoming) an employer who is willing to listen, learn, and accommodate can go a long way. While interviewing can hold many challenges under any circumstances, these types of truly welcoming, evolving workplaces are worth seeking out.

Practicing autism-friendly workplace and career advocacy, No. 3: Be aware of potential difficulties

Why is this needed?

While we certainly hope for an inclusive, supportive work environment where people of all neurologies can work meaningfully together, it's also wise to prepare for worst-case scenarios, or at least to have an understanding of common obstacles Autistic people have encountered in the workplace. Our contributors shared examples of poor workplace accommodations and having to deal with employers and employees who lacked an understanding of autism. This can encourage an unhealthy cycle of masking and meltdowns. Unsupportive work environments ultimately instigate the desire or need to change jobs, making job retention an additional challenge.

Considering community work programs

Some community work programs try to mitigate some of the common issues with initial work experiences by offering interview and job training, and helping people find work in meaningful areas that match their interests and skill sets. Ideally, they have a supportive culture that values the dignity of each person and treats them like an active participant in planning their futures.

Our contributors shared mixed feelings about these programs, with some sharing their excitement about being able to try different kinds of jobs and others feeling frustrated with the program culture. One respondent (she/her) has experience in multiple work programs; some she loved (an office program that contracted with a local hospital) and others she didn't. She says, unfortunately, the program she didn't like is more typical:

The other experience I had was more common, where I worked at a program that had adults with disabilities doing janitorial services at local businesses around town. I loved the office program, but I couldn't stand the janitorial one. There just was this weird culture of "oh look at us providing employment and independence to these people who wouldn't be employed anywhere else," yet... There were quite a few kids who used this janitorial program to earn easy money so they didn't have to try harder and make something more for themselves.

Work programs will vary widely, depending on needs and community resources, some offering full-time aides during the work day or simply helping with the job search process. Families and individuals can consider these programs as part of the career planning or transition journey, while staying mindful of the program's limitations, so we can be prepared to keep putting ourselves back "out there" (or helping the people we care about get back "out there") if Plan A doesn't work out.

Navigating poor workplace accommodations and a lack of understanding of autism

Without a suitable environment, it's impossible for people to flourish. This is true for people of all neurologies. Ideally, we find work where we won't have Bidon's (she/her) workplace experience: "Accommodations are a bloody nightmare." Once you've landed a job, you have to regularly assess the physical, social, and professional environment to determine if and when self-advocacy is necessary, how to advocate for support (if needed), and whether the job experience is worth the lack of accommodations or other challenges you might have to endure. A failure to accommodate in the workplace is often due to a lack of understanding of autism.

Day (e/em/eir) explains that it was challenging "being thrown into a world made entirely without people like me in mind." E felt unprepared and without coping mechanisms at work:

> An example is how to act around a manager at a job or how to understand my limits at a job (or even that I would have limits at a job). It sounds trivial, but these are things that have had serious impacts on my life, so far as to even cause me to become homeless.

According to one respondent (NP), autism-aware, better-educated supervisors and managers who are mindful of the needs of Autistic people and people with other disabilities could bring great improvements to the workplace. Many contributors discussed the uncomfortable and sometimes intolerable situation of working for a boss who lacks an understanding of autism.

The results can be devastating. Chloe (she/her) once worked in a bakery with an assistant manager who wasn't very understanding of her mental health. She says that she found "working in customer services as an Autistic person a complete nightmare" and describes how seriously her situation spiraled: "It caused Autistic burnout, several meltdowns, and eventually led to me trying to take my own life as I couldn't cope. I ended up admitted into a psychiatric unit." Now she works to train people about autism so they can implement more inclusive services. She's also trying to get this autism training to be co-produced and delivered by Autistic people.

Max (he/him) similarly discussed the difficulty he had with self-advocating for his communication preferences at work. He wanted someone to help communicate his specific needs, but feared it would appear unprofessional. "I think it would help young adults with autism if employers understand that we may need help communicating our needs, especially if working a new job in an unfamiliar environment," he explains.

Understanding the difficulty of retaining jobs

So many contributors shared the difficulty of keeping a job. They cited problems with how they were treated in different work environments, trying to navigate social situations, routines, and sensory stimuli in the workplace, and finding jobs that matched their interests and skill sets.

"I've been unable to keep a traditional job longer than six months," says Marsh (they/them). "It seems to be a function of forced routine and social rules more than anything else." Shekhar (she/her) had a love for teaching, and was manipulated into thinking she was applying for a teaching job, when in fact, she ended up working in sales:

> They recruited me with the promise that I would teach a certain kids' course. It was an illusion. I was to sell the course, not teach it. I wasn't good at sales, but I was told this was the first step to becoming a teacher. And I believed them. I go by words and can't read implied meanings. So I got cheated. They harassed me to no end. I was traumatized.

She eventually obtained a teaching license and a teaching job, which she loved, but still found it difficult to fit in:

> I *loved* my job. I was very good at it. I was a favourite among children and parents. My class performance was very high compared to others'... I had found my place, I thought... But...I never fitted in. I couldn't be another brick in the wall, and my being this way encouraged my students also not to be. So I was an integral threat to the schools I worked in. Since 2013, I have worked in four schools. I have been fired from three and, in the fourth one, I had to leave because I couldn't pretend to be like everybody else. I developed high anxiety and depression, trying to mask.

Day (e/em/eir) says e has had 29 jobs in ten years, averaging six to nine months per job. E shares some of the difficulties e's encountered:

> I have a lot of sensory sensitivities that severely limit a lot of my options. There's also a lot of jobs I get fired from because I need a consistent predictable schedule, but that's an extremely rare gem... Another issue is I need explicit step-by-step instructions, but bosses want a worker who will take a brief vague line of the end goal they have in mind and then expect the worker to trot off and do the

implied tasks they want. Authority also usually has issues with me when I can't figure out how to appropriately talk at work or to co-workers or customers.

Some people said they found it easier to obtain a job than it was to keep it. One respondent (she/her) says, "Getting hired hasn't been hard since I am able to put on a performance. The issue has been keeping the job." Vu (he/him) says that finding a job has been difficult, and it's hard to "keep up constantly with industry trends and learn new skills just to stay competitive in the job market." Maclean (NP) says it's been a struggle to find a job that pays enough to allow them to be independent.

Respondents who held jobs long-term cited supportive employers as a contributing factor to that enduring success. Kimble (she/her) explains, "I've had to have a lot of accommodations in order to do my job well, which my manager has been very supportive of. She's the reason I haven't left this job." Cordeiro (they/them) found a job at an animal shelter where they can perform tasks at a pace that feels right for them, thanks to understanding staff.

When it comes to the difficulties encountered by Autistic people in the workplace, ignorance among leadership and co-workers seems to be the absolute biggest factor in issues with obtaining, retaining, and feeling good about employment. It's important to be aware of this possibility while also remaining open to finding work environments with actively welcoming colleagues and managers. And readers who are in positions to improve workplace acceptance and awareness—whether for themselves or someone they care about, for a co-worker or potential hire, for a particular organization, or in general—should do everything in their power to do so.

Practicing autism-friendly workplace and career advocacy, No. 4: When appropriate, be open about your neurology

Why is this needed?

Considering disclosure in the workplace is inevitable when it comes to job planning, maintenance, and advancement. But there's no obvious or all-purpose solution. Whether or not to disclose will depend on multiple factors, including the job culture, opportunities for advancement, the length of time one is expected to stay, the risks of stereotyping and discrimination, and the specific needs of the employee, among other reasons. Our contributors shared their advice in this area, as well as strategies for supporting Autistic employees and creating more inclusive workplaces.

Considering and preparing for the perils of disclosure

The decision to disclose is complex. For Evans (he/him):

> The biggest challenge transitioning into adulthood is the decision to either do my best to keep my diagnosis a secret, or to be open about it. I fear being treated differently, which usually happens to me most of the time.

Some of our contributors substantiated Evans' fears, sharing how the idea of open or inclusive workspaces didn't play out in reality, and disclosing their diagnosis didn't help, but actually led to further scrutiny. Marsh (they/them) says:

> The idea of an open workplace where you can theoretically come to your boss with issues has caused problems more than once. The result tends to be higher scrutiny of your work and a cut in hours. It's never easy choosing whether or not to disclose.

Harrington (she/her) says, "I've been warned to stay in the closet about my disabilities while at work."

Emily (she/her) describes how she struggled with disclosure after receiving a diagnosis while she was already employed:

> I currently work full time as a graphic designer... I was three years into my job role when I found out I was Autistic, and now I feel if I tell my employer, it will change their opinion of me despite the fact I can do my job and do it well, with high-quality output. Before the pandemic, I worked in an open-plan office five days a week, and it was hugely burning me out due to the sensory input constantly surrounding me.

Unfortunately, when considering disclosure, Autistic employees usually have to weigh the possibility of stereotyping, patronization, underestimation, questions around competence, or even social isolation.

Considering the benefits of disclosure

The encouraging news is that many of our contributors reported positive experiences with being open about their neurology! One respondent (she/her) says she has always been honest about her neurodivergence, even though "the hardest place has been in the workplace, especially because it's a social and fast-paced environment, filled with lights and sounds, and if you're in hospitality and retail, you find out very fast it's you vs. workplace." This respondent has learned to be honest and work hard "and then when you hit your personal limit, you must stop." She warns, "Don't fall for the 'put 110 percent in'... it'll ruin you. Put in the 100 percent, then put your foot down. Be your own cheerleader and your own bouncer."

Truty (she/her) says:

> It's important for an employer to know what challenges their people are bringing to the job... I've always been open

about the things I'm not comfortable with or when I really need a day off because I've overtaxed myself. They know about things like my migraines, the severe medication for my rheumatoid arthritis, my sources of anxiety, and my absolute disdain for fluorescent lights. Luckily, we're all able to work around that so I'm able to use my skills to forward our shared goals.

Hall (she/her) explained how her fellow staff were "beyond incredible," and her waitressing boss was willing to offer accommodations. She was allowed to listen to headphones while clearing tables to block out noise. Hall said he told her that although "he may not know everything about autism, I could comfortably explain if there was ever an issue I needed help with surrounding my autism and my job."

Abramowski (she/her) shared how being openly Autistic has made her more of an asset to her positions as a behavior management coordinator, a direct support professional, and a residential assistant because she is able to relate to the people she works with and feels valued by her employers: "It was known I was autistic when I interviewed for a position at the autism agency I work in on a relief basis, and it's been great being both a self-advocate and an employee!"

Sara (she/her) has benefited from a support group she started to connect with other neurodivergent co-workers:

Best. Move. Ever...those who identify as neurodivergent and those who simply want to be allies working together to educate the rest of the company. While it's still in its infancy, we don't feel the need to explain ourselves to each other. If someone needs an accommodation, they speak up, and it isn't questioned.

If people are experiencing stress or burnout, vocalizing these issues can be helpful, says Macedo (he/him), and he asks employers to take these requests seriously. Disclosing a diagnosis can potentially lead to a more aware, accepting, accommodating (physically, psychologically, and socially) atmosphere, and thus a more productive, meaningful, and enjoyable work environment.

Conclusion: Creating inclusive workplaces

Working or would-be working Autistic people, NT/ND employers, and NT employees wanting to improve inclusivity (which includes everyone, we hope!) can consider the advice of our contributors, some of whom have professional and personal experience both as employees in different work settings and as leaders of universal design in the workplace. Cohen (she/her) says that "having rules to follow, a role and purpose, and being needed has always been helpful for and desired by me."

At Ultranauts, Ciampi (she/her) has seen the positive impact of bonding within a truly inclusive workspace. The organization has paid "community gatherings" where everyone has the chance to discuss what's working and what isn't in the work culture, "such as feeling a sense of belonging at work as a member of the LGBTQIA+ community, upcoming performance reviews, trends, and other topics." She says:

> What's interesting is that before Covid, the national average for people feeling lonely at work was 40 percent, and at Ultranauts it was always 10 percent; but during Covid, our "feeling lonely at work" numbers actually dropped to 5 percent. So the company and employer community is communicating inclusivity. People feel they belong, that they're connected, and they're reporting feelings of less loneliness and less isolation.

Ciampi (she/her) explains:

Universal design and inclusivity are about looking at a

broken workplace system that we've had for over 100 years, and revamping it, giving it a tune-up, a new look, so that it can be more inclusive and give underrepresented groups a chance at true liberty.

This doesn't have to be an expensive, complex process. Easy-to-implement practices could include:

- holding virtual interviews.
- clearly communicating job expectations and processes.
- conducting regular check-ins with employees.
- eliminating mobility barriers with work-from-home options.

Positive change in this area starts with an interest in being equitable and inclusive, sharing suggestions for improvement and inquiring about how you can improve, and a willingness to openly communicate and listen.

SUMMARY GUIDANCE:
#ActuallyAutistic practical tips for work and career success

- Consider part-time and full-time, and remote and on-site, work opportunities.
- Think about other job environmental factors such as the potential for travel or length of work day.
- Remember that research and self-inquiry are vital parts of the job search process for many Autistic people.
- Consider requesting a virtual interview if that might be more comfortable for you or the person you care about. Employers/managers should consider offering this option.
- Plan how you (or someone you care about) will

showcase your/their work skills and experience before attending an interview.

- Research community work programs.
- Consider the potential pitfalls and benefits of workplace disclosure.
- [For ND and NT employers/managers] Offer clear roles, rules, and policies to follow. [For ND and NT employees] Seek a workplace that offers clear roles, rules, and policies, and advocate for them in your current place of employment.
- [For ND and NT employees] Look for jobs with inclusive leaders who explicitly cultivate an agile, adaptive, open, caring, welcoming work culture and a flexible, welcoming built environment, and advocate for these in your workplace. [For ND and NT employers/managers] Regularly check in with employees to assess their contentment and needs; express your openness to conversations about inclusively evolving the workplace (in terms of culture, built environment, and so on) and meeting workers' specific needs. Follow through on those findings.

REFLECTION QUESTIONS

? How can you (or the people you care about) best prepare for a job interview? What are some potential barriers to interview success and what might mitigate them?

? What are the key factors you (or the people you care about) should consider in your (their) unique job search? Include your (their) needs and skills, as well as various aspects of potential career paths (such as required credentials, opportunities for advancement, weekly hours required, and compensation) and workplaces (including sensory environment, location, accessibility, culture, etc.).

? Under what conditions would you (or the one you care about) be comfortable disclosing an autism diagnosis in a job-search or work context? Are there any resources (people, programs, etc.) you can leverage to help your disclosure be a positive experience?

? [For ND and NT employers/managers] How do/can you incorporate inclusive design practices into your recruitment and hiring processes? How do/can you incorporate inclusive design practices into the everyday work culture of your organization?

? [For ND and NT employers/managers] What are you doing to learn more about neurodiversity and evaluate your organization's work practices and processes? [For ND and NT employees and potential employees] How can you learn more about neurodiversity (including your own neurodivergence, where applicable) in ways that will benefit your career, co-workers (or future co-workers), and workplace (or future workplace)?

? Can you (or the people you care about) bring your (their) whole self to work? How about the people you (they) work with?

Step 8

Develop Truly Welcoming Public Spaces

Demand that public spaces at least sometimes create a space for us to exist, too.

—DAY (E/EM/EIR)

Independence in part rests on access. Being able to make our own choices with autonomy means we can follow up on the major and minor decisions we make. It means we can do what we need and want to do. This will often involve activities outside the home, such as dining out, obtaining medical care, socializing, working, shopping, enjoying the outdoors, attending events and meetings, and so on.

Yet many of the spaces these activities occur in can be physically, sensorially, emotionally, and psychologically unwelcoming for Autistic people. And when going places feels daunting, freedom diminishes on many levels, including the freedoms to accomplish one's goals, make friends, pursue wellness, enjoy recreational activities, and purchase things one needs, among others. Hope itself—for the future, for personal and professional growth—is inherently tied to the ability to go where you need and want to go and do what you need and want to do. Thus, public environments that overwhelm or discriminate against or exclude us may not only deprive us of necessities and opportunities, they may affect our mental health, causing despair, isolation, shutdowns, meltdowns, burnout, and more.

So locating inclusive spaces is definitely important in the quest for increased independence. But finding ways to make all spaces more inclusive is also vital, since we all typically need to go to the dentist, obtain food, access transportation—regardless of whether these services, offices, and so on are actively welcoming where we live. We all also have the fundamental right to participate in the benefits of public goods, such as parks and libraries.

As one respondent (she/her) noted regarding our survey query about improving community spaces, "This is a difficult question. There are so many different people and so many different needs." Nonetheless, the effort to improve access and inclusion in shared public spaces is an imperative for equality, equity, and autonomy.

Day (e/em/eir) has some fabulous suggestions for where to start:

Normalize stores by having a sensory-free day—hell, even an hour!—where they dim the lights and turn off the radios and mute the registers and carts. Color code the carts/baskets, having one be a "Leave me alone" color and another an "I'm fine to talk to" color. Train cashiers in how to not panic or get upset if somebody doesn't respond to their sales pitches (and maybe give them an hour to not have to give sales pitches). Have time-out zones in cafes, libraries, and so on, that are completely quiet and have lots of stim toys. Ask us for our input when making public spaces in general.

Making sure we all can enter the physical space/environment

What do you (or the Autistic people you care about) need to feel physically welcome and sensorially comfortable? Consider factors beyond basic physical accessibility. Take an inventory of spaciousness, ease of navigation, crowds, lights, sounds, and scents. Perhaps, like Maclean (NP), physical tools for grounding and proprioception, including "an area for us to feel the walls," are helpful in public spaces. Maclean also suggests headphones and sunglasses to ease sensory overload. One respondent (NP) points to physical environments that tone down the light, sound, and so on (more on this below): "A lot of shops and community places around me have a quiet hour where they turn lights down and don't play music. That's nice I think."

Ensuring everyone feels comfortable in psychological/emotional environments and cultures

What do you need to feel safe and welcome when you enter and spend time in a space? How can we feel like we belong? Cordeiro (they/them) suggests banning bigotry: "[Welcoming spaces] have a zero-tolerance policy for discrimination." Forrester (any/varies) advocates for no judgment, noting that "It's helpful when adults don't cast withering glances at parents whose children are 'acting out'"; this holds true for "withering glances" of any sort—toward anyone.

Moody (she/her) describes a space that seems on point for both physical-sensory and cultural-emotional inclusion:

> In my town, we have a local library. This library does very well including everyone through their interactive digital activities and their in-the-building activities. They also

have ramps and accessible systems. One example of this is their online library system, which means you can have books delivered digitally, in the library itself, or even through their new mobile library, which comes to your house and delivers the books.

Adulthood won't look the same for everybody, but we believe everybody is entitled to access and benefit from public spaces. The following are five ways to design and improve public spaces to promote access for Autistic people. As a bonus, many of these practices—like lots of the suggestions in this book—promote unconditional inclusivity, and thus hold true for diverse populations in general.

Developing welcoming public spaces, No. 1: Design quiet spaces for work and socializing

Why is this needed?

Sensory sensitivities and processing differences are a facet of neurodivergence experienced by most Autistic people. But quiet is also an emotional and social need for many, an essential state that enables us to self-regulate and recharge. For our survey respondents, sound was the most common sensory vulnerability, and space to be alone or not too crowded was a frequently expressed need. So, when asked what truly inclusive environments are like, many mentioned opportunities for solitude, silence, or low noise as a requirement. For Marsh (they/them), for example, "It would have to be a quiet place with lots of different activity options."

Honoring diverse auditory needs

Baik (she/her) is reluctant to speak "on behalf of other people's disabilities or circumstances," but shares that, in her opinion, "anywhere that isn't too noisy is inclusive." Bidon (she/her) adds the option for solitude as a good addition to inclusive public spaces: "Quiet spaces for one person only. Should be soundproof so they can be alone." For one respondent (she/her), a quiet space could provide an outlet for frustration. The demands of her full-time job give her "the urge to find a quiet place" where she can let off steam by stimming in privacy.

Facilitating communication

Auditory needs also encompass non-speaking communication modes. So inclusive quiet spaces (along with inclusive spaces in general) may also support and enable non-spoken communication, as one respondent details: "sensory friendly, and with options that don't necessitate verbal communication." Chloe (she/her) concurs:

> ...quieter spaces, less brightness of lights, no loud tannoy systems [known as "loudspeakers" in the U.S.], have devices where people can communicate easier so it's more inclusive of non-speaking Autistic people, and there should be a variety of different communication ways understood and used.

Designating separate areas

Creating public spaces where one can find ways to be alone to recharge, and where it's possible to engage in an activity without too much auditory input, enables people of all neurologies to participate. Welcoming public spaces may choose to offer different areas for different functions, with some spaces designated as silent and/or limited to fewer people. As Marsh (they/them) notes, quiet places could "include a separate area for working and socializing. Bookstores aren't bad for this sort of thing."

Emily (she/her) celebrates two places that meet many people's need for silence:

> I would say libraries and bookshops tend to be the most inclusive spaces because they never play background music

and tend to be more dimly lit, which makes them more inviting. They are also usually quite clearly labelled spaces, which make wayfinding much easier. Also, I think there is a (lovely) assumption that you have to be quiet when you enter these spaces, which to me is great!

Developing welcoming public spaces, No. 2: Create sensory-friendly environments

Why is this needed?

Our respondents echo the many Autistic, otherwise ND, and/or highly sensitive people who have expressed the need for certain sensory updates and adaptations to enable their well-being in public spaces. When public spaces assault their physiology, Autistic people quite simply cannot take part in the basic public goods and services those spaces offer. In such spaces, they either *cannot* learn, shop, eat out, attend events, work, and so on, or they do so at great personal cost, including anxiety, migraines, meltdowns, and exhaustion.

Being actively welcoming around sensory needs

To create truly inclusive sensory environments, we must honor our own experience and/or listen to the Autistic people in our lives. As Corrado (she/her) says, "I think people need to talk to autistic persons about creating a sensory-accommodating environment that is empathetic to autistic persons"; she herself suggests "a sensory-friendly space that has fewer people." Even designating certain days as less jarring to the senses can be a good start toward inclusivity, as Birch (she/her) points out: "Make things sensory-friendly. Have a day once a month where the lights are dimmer and the music is lower."

Tino (he/him) suggests developing community spaces that are calm, dim, and quiet, as well as spacious:

...so you have room to move and be away from too many

people. To me, a room is better with softer lighting. I don't like fluorescent lights. If there are acoustic tiles and carpet, I am able to tolerate sound better.

Abramowski (she/her) thinks a great welcoming space would offer certain amenities: "It would be accessible to people of all abilities, and have places for sensory breaks. Fidgets and earplugs would be available for those who need them. All would be welcome!"

Developing welcoming public spaces, No. 3: Be sure all spaces are accessible

Why is this needed?

Our respondents noted that public inclusivity obviously entails adhering to local laws, and providing for things like "physically accessible spaces and quiet spaces" (Cordeiro, they/them). For example, in the U.S., that should entail being "actually ADA [Americans with Disabilities Act] compatible, not just a ramp in an awkward location" (Birch, she/her).

But many disability accommodations that are required under various countries' disability protections are not designed for, or helpful to, Autistic people. And because autism is in some ways an *invisible* difference, it's not always obvious when a particular Autistic person encounters obstacles in a specific environment. In fact, many, many barriers to Autistic access still exist—and can and should be addressed, whether under the law (see Stage Four, our online resource on the Jessica Kingsley website, for more ideas and tips on legal matters) or simply because it's the right thing to do.

The social model of disability provides moral and practical justification for meeting the needs of all disabled people/ people with differences. This model is based on the premise that the responsibility for a lack of access never lies with the person themselves, but with certain facets of physical and social environments that are *disabling* to people with differences. These barriers to independence, access, and success must be abolished. One respondent (she/they) expresses this truth eloquently:

> I think that most disabilities are only viewed as such because the "normal" standard is so much accepted and every minority seems to be oppressed. In my opinion, that is what makes life unfair for disabled people, because there simply isn't enough accommodation and acceptance for differences. The problem is seen as the person not being able to do something, rather than as society failing to accommodate their differences. I think that even just caring about that person is a good thing, and that being respectful and just asking a person about their preferences and needs is key to helping them.

Access may also involve explicitly offering the option—and perhaps even a designated area—to take whatever physical or mental space one needs to self-regulate. Nied (she/they) explains:

> Some of my biggest barriers in regards to work and volunteering are environmental... I require time to acclimate to a space. I need to know what's around me, even if I work in that space many times a week, I need to maybe touch things that are familiar so I ground myself with where I am, and, if need be, just step outside, or go to a quiet space if too many people are talking at once, so I can reset.

Ensuring physical, sensory, emotional, and psychological accessibility

The necessary support and accommodations for the physical-cultural-social spaces that make up our public environments can take many forms, from welcoming "service animals and disability aids" (Cordeiro, they/them) to providing opportunities to meet a person's sensory or proprioceptive needs. In addition, as Birch (she/her) suggests, supportive spaces should not deploy stereotypes around disability or neurodivergence: "No profiling."

Independence can't exist without access. Including diverse perspectives, including those of Autistic people, when conceiving, designing, renovating, and updating public spaces, is key to making those spaces genuinely accessible.

Developing welcoming public spaces, No. 4: Seek and train knowledgeable staff

Why is this needed?
True inclusivity is largely based on the predominant culture in a given environment. That tone starts with staff. Autism-friendly, neuro-affirming, intersectionality-welcoming spaces—be they stores, restaurants, medical and therapeutic practices, schools, libraries, banks, corporations, non-profits, local businesses, or any other organizations and spaces—keep DEI (diversity, equity, and inclusion) at the forefront of their hiring and training processes.

Avoiding harm, promoting wellness
Knowledgeable staff will promote and support the autonomy of those who come into their purview, while ignorant or uncaring staff can have a significant negative impact. This is particularly true of medical and educational settings. Day (e/em/eir) suggests:

> For the love of all that is holy, please, please, PLEASE, train teachers, doctors, nurses, hospital staff, dentists, and so on how to have an autistic patient/student! Hospitals and going to the dentist are hell because they cause meltdowns every time and not a single medical person knows how to not make things worse. They should know more than others, but they don't know anything at all usually.

As Bridge suggests, welcoming "leaders/designers/administrators" of inclusive spaces "are reflective and accountable when they make mistakes." Businesses, non-profits, schools, and other organizations can grow, just like people can. Ongoing training can bring all employees up to date on best practices for inclusivity.

Weldon (she/her), a naturopathic physician and former health coach, underscores the importance of implementing awareness and acceptance in the environments and cultures of any profession that seeks to serve people of all neurologies (abilities, genders, ethnicities, sexual orientations, ages...):

> Wellness should be accessible for us all: chronically ill, disabled, aging, neurodivergent, sensitive, mentally ill, Black and Brown, queer, trans, non-binary, soft, sparkly, and matte ;-). There is no one right way to be well or take care of ourselves. What we each need to be able to answer "How are you?" with an honest "I'm well!" is unique, and my work is to help people redefine wellness in a way that is sustainable and fits with each individual's experience and daily life. I celebrate the possibility of being autistic and well, disabled and well... Embracing a neurodiversity paradigm in medicine means accepting that all differences are not pathological, even when those differences may also be disabilities that deserve accommodation and support, such as autism.

The benefits gained in public spaces—fundamental rights, such as healthcare; basic tools for life, such as employment, volunteering, grocery shopping; and social pursuits, such as entertainment and outdoor recreation—are all integral, necessary facets of independence and personal and professional growth. That means the staff in such spaces must be—or learn to be—accepting, aware, and genuinely supportive of all who enter their domain.

Hiring and employing intersectional people

What should employees in inclusive spaces look like? According to Cordeiro (they/them), "They look like a staff that understand and communicate openly about disability, without it being taboo. These staff should include disabled folks with no exceptions."

It seems obvious that places serving diverse populations (i.e., every place, right?) should hire and train diverse staff. But Bridge (they/them) gives an example of how rare this practice can be, even in overtly intersectional spaces:

A few community programs I was involved with trained queer and trans youth in how to give workshops on issues queer and trans youth face. It was great in giving skills to a bunch of youth, but those who managed to get through the training ended up being mostly white, university educated LGB, trans men, and AFAB [assigned female at birth] non-binary folks. I was the only trans woman of colour to get through for a while.

Perhaps the best way to ensure diverse staffing is to rely on diverse leadership, offering management roles to qualified people who are likely to make inclusive hiring choices.

When management and employees are knowledgeable, accepting, and open to adapting a space to meet people's needs, that space is exponentially more likely to feel welcoming to Autistic people (among others!). And being able to see yourself reflected in the places you go is another wonderful thing. It gives people with differences, including Autistic people, both hope and confidence.

Developing welcoming public spaces, No. 5: Practice inclusive planning

Why is this needed?

Spaces work best for all when being welcoming to all is part of the original purpose and design, not an afterthought. It's easier, and perhaps in some cases better, to bake inclusivity in from the start. This means being proactive about a variety of potentially relevant barriers to entry, such as avoiding fluorescent lights, creating designated quiet spaces, and using inclusive hiring practices (as above), right at the outset. It could mean that online or delivery options are integral to the business model from the beginning, improving access for those with limited mobility and/or social and/or sensory capacities.

Of course, now is always the best time to start evolving. Planning that encompasses inclusive adaptations will benefit any space at any stage! Such planning needn't be limited to the concerns of Autistic people, but should certainly include them. As Bridge (they/them) notes, people intentionally planning, designing, or updating welcoming spaces naturally take diverse needs into account: "They think about common needs for a bunch of groups and make it part of the production of their space. They support folks from many communities."

Listening when planning

Welcoming public spaces incorporate respectful, active listening into decision-making processes. In Chloe's (she/her) words:

> I think people need to listen to Autistic and disabled people better and include us in decisions and conversations about Autism and disabilities. Also for us to be able to co-produce and co-deliver training or presentations, and for us to be involved in the creation and planning of things

for Autistic people...whether that be products, services, and so on. Autistic people should and *must* be included. We need our voices to be centered more. We need people to listen, understand.

Honoring Autistic voices, along with those of all potential participants, patients, students, clients, customers, and so on, at the planning stages of any endeavor will result in public spaces that foster equality, equity, and independence.

Conclusion: Evolving public spaces for the public good

In welcoming environments, we are encouraged to ask for what we need and we can expect to be treated as equals. Vaughan (she/her) insists on what she needs to gain access and succeed: "I expect support and accommodations," she says. Not everyone is able to or feels comfortable expressing their needs in the public sphere though, so, whenever possible, we need to stick up for each other and for inclusivity, so that everyone can make their own choices and live their lives with as much independence as possible.

However, proactively inclusive spaces can reduce or eliminate the need to ask to have our needs met by incorporating diverse voices and needs throughout their planning, hiring, training, strategy, design, and change/updating processes, and by comprehensively weaving inclusivity into their culture. Such spaces will integrate amenities such as quiet areas, sensory-friendly practices, options for non-speaking communication, online options for participation, and delivery services into their organizational model. In these ways, we can evolve public spaces into places where Autistic people can flourish.

SUMMARY GUIDANCE:
#ActuallyAutistic practical tips for creating welcoming public spaces

- Autistic people's wellness, personal growth, social and career success, and basic independence depend on inclusive environments, making evolving such spaces a matter of public health. Whatever role you play, begin to think about how things could be improved.
- Physical, sensory, cultural, interpersonal, and emotional elements of public spaces all matter when it comes to genuine access.
- Integrating intersectional perspectives at all levels of staffing and in all life stages of public spaces vastly increases accessibility and inclusivity. Take surveys, host focus groups, and hire neurodivergent and otherwise diverse people in positions of authority in order to gain—and benefit from—a range of perspectives.
- [For ND and NT business/organization owners/management] Consider implementing quiet hours or designating quiet spaces for patrons (employees, students, patients, clients, customers, etc.) who might be overwhelmed in loud, busy environments. [For ND and NT patrons] Advocating for such updates will benefit not just you and the Autistic people you care about, but many others.
- [For ND and NT business/organization owners/management] Consider how lighting may be affecting your patrons (employees, students, patients, clients, customers, etc.) and ways you can address it (replacing fluorescent lights, dimming lights, designing spaces to take advantage of natural light, etc.). [For ND and NT patrons] As above, advocating for more inclusive lighting will inspire adaptations that help lots of people feel more at ease.

REFLECTION QUESTIONS

? What are some barriers to access you've encountered in public spaces and what might mitigate them?

? Where have you encountered welcoming public spaces and what made them so?

? What sensory or other adaptations do you find most helpful when out in the public realm?

? Does advocating for inclusive public spaces feel like "asking for too much"? Why or why not? Do you believe that adapting to diverse needs makes public spaces more welcoming to everyone?

? What local resources (whether people or organizations) might have ideas or clout for inclusively evolving local spaces?

? How can we best promote our own or others' independence in a range of public places?

Conclusion

*Accept that I have difficulties with some things, but at the
same time, don't think I am incapable of certain things just
because I am autistic.*

—ANONYMOUS (SHE/THEY)

Similar to the progression of advocacy advice in our last book,
we've explored building independence starting with the most
personal level and expanding through schools and workplaces
and communities all the way up to the societal and global
scales (the latter are covered extensively in Stage Four, our
online resource). Relying on input from more than 100 Autistic teens, young adults, and adults, we've proposed actions,
mindsets, tweaks, and updates that support Autistic people
in transitioning to greater autonomy.

We hope we've helped empower people to shape their own
destiny via actions—such as participating in trainings, finding
resources, working hard, creating reminders, and so on—and
mindsets—such as the conviction that we are all worthy of
respect, the belief that we can all grow healthier and happier,
and so on.

We've also tried to show that relying on others is simply
a part of life for all humans to a greater or lesser degree. As
Kmarie (prefers not to use pronouns) notes, "One of my biggest

lessons was embracing interdependence. I realized that while I'm independent in some aspects, in others I need community."

Other factors, including cultures, relationships, policies and laws, institutions, and built environments, also shape who we are and how we evolve. In this book, we have covered many practical options for shifting those factors in ways that better enable Autistic young people and adults to make their own choices and strive toward and achieve their goals.

Let's be very clear: we are not looking to demonize, denigrate, or silence anyone whose perspectives we have not included here, whether that's neurotypical people or Autistic or otherwise neurodivergent people we haven't communicated with through our research. We respect various viewpoints and our hope is that they can co-exist without the need to judge.

What we do hold unequivocally true is that Autistic people—with all of their full humanity, perspectives, needs, dreams, hopes, differences, goals—need and deserve respect, inclusion, and acceptance. But since we don't always get what we need and deserve, despite the fact that these things are typically required for healthy daily life and growth, we've leaned on abundant input from our research to develop actionable ways we can create small and large shifts to enable Autistic people to flourish as they take crucial steps toward adulthood at any age.

Creating welcoming schools and homes where we can build strengths, gain knowledge, and feel cared for and comfortable

Stage One covered the most intimate spaces in which Autistic people live, learn, and grow. We showed how, as the source of healthy self-esteem, confidence, and stability, a truly inclusive home and family life can provide vital nourishment for Autistic youth and adults. Autism-affirming, broadly welcoming homes serve as a refuge and safe space to heal and recover from the sensory and emotional challenges of the outside world, while also empowering residents to dream big—and pursue those dreams on their own timeline. These homes can serve as a model of a shared, lived practice of intersectional acceptance, interdependence, continuous learning, justice, honesty, openness, and trust. They are also spaces where people can learn to have hard conversations in a respectful way. And they serve as a solid, reliable launching pad for any and all efforts toward independence.

For all of these reasons, having a home where they are unconditionally loved and embraced—where they "feel accepted and engaged...around others who take me as I am" (Abramowski, she/her), and where "people treat me like anyone else, and respect my boundaries around the things about me that are 'strange' when I ask them to" (Nora, she/her)—matters deeply to our respondents.

That's not to say that everybody comes from such a home. We encourage anyone who feels there's room for improvement in their home life to delve deeper into the ideas and suggestions found in Step 1. This goes for people who are still living in their family homes as well as for those in other living situations. The tips in this chapter can help at any stage and in any home context.

Outside the home, Autistic people sometimes struggle to find ways to interact with others, especially after high school. But making sustainable connections and seeking out enjoyable, accessible activities are other key parts of independence. Our respondents made it clear that there are almost infinite options for relationships and activities, from online meet-ups and gaming, to face-to-face connections formed around mutual interests. Many mentioned the relative ease and comfort of forming friendships with other Autistic people. They also discussed less traditional pursuits and relationship choices. And they insisted that we should not feel pressure to mask just to "fit in." It may take a little effort or patience or openness to new ways of communicating, but there are friends out there for everyone. Steps 2 and 3 offered many suggestions around interpersonal, social, and recreational possibilities, based on our respondents' experiences and wisdom.

In Step 4, we integrated a whole lot of frank advice from our respondents into a comprehensive overview of the ways middle and high schools are both serving and letting down Autistic students—and proposed concrete solutions based on Autistic students' experiences. We hope all students can access the type of classrooms Shekhar (she/her) recommends, "where the environment makes them happy, passionate, and able to access a high-quality life." And we hope more and more teachers learn to celebrate and nurture what makes each student unique, like those Kimble (she/her) describes: "My favorite teachers were always the ones who understood me a little better than the rest. They knew I was different and would help me embrace that. They also loved my art too, and my love for animals."

Step 4 offered sensible, proactive ways to make schools more inclusive and adaptive, so that all students can learn and grow. We agree wholeheartedly with Kronby's (they/them) view that "everyone should be able to gain access to supports to get a degree without being interrogated, invalidated, or just simply told no."

Once again, it all comes down to basic respect, built on the assumption that all people are worthy of genuine inclusion and are able to learn, whatever their support, sensory, or other needs. We shared tips for classrooms (including vocational and homeschool settings), schedules, deadlines, materials, teaching, and more. We also made suggestions for open and autism-affirming school activities, from ways to build awareness/acceptance of autism, disability, and intersectionality to welcoming after-school programs. And we described options for both anti-bullying and pro-friend-making efforts. When middle and high schools actually prepare students for their next steps, they enter young adulthood stronger and with more tools to tackle their goals, fight adversity, and reach for their dreams.

Fostering healthy, successful transitions toward independence

The post-high school years are often incredibly challenging for Autistic young people. There are many reasons for this. Many face a lack of a clear path forward, unless they are very confident about and suited to a certain academic niche or school, subject of study/training, or career. While high school can be a mix of both positive and negative daily interactions, the sudden cessation of daily social interaction—however forced—can result in loneliness. The instant reduction in or termination of supportive services that occurs in most countries just after high school ends can be another daunting obstacle. And since Autistic youth may mature on their own timelines, expectations around the increased responsibilities and decisions of adulthood may feel particularly burdensome.

In Stage Two, we discussed this extremely important and complex period at length. Refer back to Step 5 for tips on transition services, managing feelings, specific changes, and more if you are (or the person you care about is) a recent graduate or graduating in the next few years. Step 6 is about making decisions and taking proactive measures when it comes to concrete options, such as college, internships, volunteering, and work. It also covered driving—a complicated issue for many Autistic people. Finally, Step 6 delved into various aspects of independent living possibilities, from increased responsibility and autonomy in the family home to living on one's own or with a partner or roommate.

In Steps 5 and 6, we covered the practical side, such as how to find supportive learning, workplace, or independent-living resources, as well as more personal and emotional aspects, including insights for cultivating an accepting mindset on the varied paths people take toward learning, work, and independence.

We've tried to cover just about every possible area involved in independence, so readers can be aware of things they might not otherwise take into account. As always, we and our respondents counsel an open attitude and frank discussion or self-reflection around skills and strengths, as well as regarding where research and scaffolding might be necessary or helpful. With a caring and positive attitude, it's possible to navigate these big transitions in a healthy way.

Developing communities and workplaces that empower Autistic people to thrive

Stage Three went deeper into the spaces where Autistic young adults and adults seek to work, live their daily lives, and socialize. We concluded that targeted advocacy in these spaces would vastly improve young adult and adult life for Autistic people—and others, too. We came up with specific areas where updates are needed and made suggestions for how to go about making the necessary changes.

Work is often a central part of adult life, both in terms of personal achievement and satisfaction and in giving us the ability to contribute or support ourselves financially. But finding and keeping a suitable job can be one of the biggest struggles Autistic young people (and adults) face. So, we offered extensive tips from our respondents on choosing work that's a good fit, as well as on navigating workplace dynamics, from interviews and disclosure to organizational cultures.

Our communities are also integral to independence—and they can uplift us or keep us down. We explored several main aspects of welcoming communities, from sensory updates to intersectionality education for staff in public-facing roles, whether that means librarians, restaurant servers, park rangers, cashiers, or anything else.

Accessibility in workplaces and communities is crucial for everyone. When all people can participate in a community, the people who live in that community all benefit. Similarly, when all employees are able to give their best efforts, organizations and their clientele prosper. Open, well-designed, informed, and accepting public spaces enable Autistic people to be themselves, do their best work, contribute meaningfully, participate fully, and live their best and most independent lives.

Honoring core principles to promote autonomy and acceptance

We believe, as we have stated many times, that autism rights and acceptance are an incredibly important aspect of social justice. In a time of such widespread social and political unrest, most civil rights movements have progressed in some ways and experienced pushback and devolution in others. Like these other movements, individual and group efforts to advance personal, social, legal, and political awareness and acceptance of neurodiversity and autism have had recent ups and downs. But, along with our respondents, readers, and many, many others, we continue to work and hope for change. (See Stage Four, our online resource, to learn about #ActuallyAutistic perspectives on social justice and get tools to promote Autistic civil rights.)

Many civil rights movements encompass differences that may be more "visible" than autism. Nonetheless, this "invisible" difference is generally a *perceivable* one. People do notice differences in most Autistic people, but may attribute them to a variety of other "causes." Unfortunately, that often leads people to behave in othering or discriminatory ways, making Autistic people one of the most marginalized groups on earth.

Raymond (he/him) describes his experiences with cruelty and discrimination—and how he uses these painful incidents to empower himself toward continued growth and advocacy:

When people found out I had Asperger's, they constantly called me retarded and wrote me off as a loon. They thought I was mentally incapable of doing anything... Really, I try not to feed into what those people say, since I know who I am at the core, and their opinions are just opinions. What they say does not define me. I continue to use that as fuel to push myself and silence all the naysayers.

One of our main points is that thinking in discriminatory, incorrect, harmful ways *harms everyone*—and that greater inclusion and acceptance *benefit everyone*. It's simply neither decent nor kind to judge people for their identity or neurology.

The guidance in all of our work—gleaned from our interviews and surveys involving hundreds of people, as well as our own experience—comes down to a core perspective on inclusion, acceptance, neurodiversity, and diversity in general. It can be summed up in the notion that while Autistic people do diverge from non-Autistic people in a variety of ways, these ways of being do not represent a deficit or problem. Instead, Autistic people embody one way of human being among many—and are thus an integral part of the human world.

So while they may present differently on an interpersonal level or have different support needs, may use an ACC device to communicate, or stay away from fluorescent lights, and so on, these differences represent not an extraordinary problem, but simply another manifestation of human diversity. Everybody has needs; neurotypical society is just better set up to meet the needs of neurotypical people—and can be disabling to those with differences. By integrating the updates outlined in this book, we can include, adapt, and accommodate people's varied needs without resorting to a disease or deficit model of autism.

We can recognize the wholeness of each person, while affirming their goals and rights around both independence and interdependence. As Cohen (she/her) points out, we are simply asking to be seen as valuable just as we are. And if we do need help, getting that support—one human to another—will actually make the world better for all. She suggests:

> Honesty and acceptance rather than trying to make an autistic person change to what is expected/considered normal. Help them focus on their strengths and use them in a productive, fulfilling way. Ask them what they want, what is important to them, and, if they do not know, be patient in helping them to figure it out.

Lucy (she/her) envisions a space where Autistic intersectionality is seen as nourishing, productive, and vital:

> I think at the autistic table, there's room for everyone; we need autistic allies, we need autistic people in medical fields, in creative fields, in advocacy groups. We need to hear more from autistic and disabled people of colour and the LGBTQ+ community, the two demographics that are the least helped and diagnosed, as well as disabled and autistic people of all ages.

We celebrate and amplify the people, including self-advocates, advocates, allies, and accomplices, who share such welcoming perspectives and refuse to settle for less than full inclusion every day and in every way. As we mentioned in the introduction, the practical details of adulthood are important, but feeling healthy and whole, and living successfully according to one's unique goals and skills, rest in large part on having people in your life who really live with acceptance, fairness, caring, and respect.

Transitions to adulthood are different for every Autistic person. Various interpersonal, social, practical, and other aspects of building independence may be more or less relevant or important depending on whose adulthood journey we're talking about. And along with their unique skills, talents, character traits, and needs, each person will have their own timeline, dreams, and goals. We believe the advances recommended in this book will help uplift and empower Autistic youth and adults to realize their goals and dreams—and thereby create more equity, equality, and even joy for them, the people who care about them, and anyone who cares about living in a more just world.

Appendix A

Survey

Short form

1. What sorts of experiences have you had in high school and what would make things better?
2. What do you find challenging about transitioning into young adulthood and what would make things better?
3. What sorts of experiences are you having (or expecting) with higher education, training, volunteering, and work, and what would make things better?
4. What sorts of actions do you think people can take to improve life for Autistic teens and young adults?

Long form

A. School experiences

1. As an Autistic student (maybe with other learning disabilities), how has your learning experience at school been? What, if anything, can make it better or easier?
2. Do you find it hard to make friends and communicate with others? What, if anything, will help you?
3. What is your favorite teacher (or any member of the school staff) like?

4. What are some things others have done or said in school that make you feel left out or uncomfortable?
5. What, if anything, has your school given you to help you learn? Are they helpful?
6. What does a classroom that includes everyone look like?
7. How can after-school activities (clubs and sports) include everyone?
8. Do you think your school helps everyone learn to accept Autism and disabilities? Why or why not?
9. What (if any) school rules or policies do you view as discriminatory against your neurodiversity or other marginalized identities (e.g., race)?

B. Transition to adulthood

1. How do you feel when you think about graduating from high school? What, if anything, can make your graduation easier?
2. If you are graduating soon or recently graduated, what are your plans for your next steps (such as working, volunteering, going to school, or something else)? Tell us about your hopes and challenges in making this change, and what might help you through.
3. If you are going (or planning to go) to school after high school (such as college or trade school), what do you think is going to be good or hard about it?
4. If you want to work or are currently working (volunteering, apprenticing, and interning count, too), what has it been like finding and keeping a job? Are you getting any employment support?
5. Do you have or want to get a driver's license? Do you find driving hard?
6. If you want or hope to do so, what can help you live on your own?

C. Autistic lived experiences

1. Have people done things with a good intention to include you, but they don't really work? Tell us about that.
2. What do community spaces (such as library, shopping mall, restaurant) that include everyone look like?
3. Tell us what it's like for you to start and grow friendships with non-Autistic people.
4. Do you worry about strangers thinking that you're weird, different, or even dangerous? Tell us about that.
5. Tell us what makes you feel accepted and included.

D. Autistic advocacy

1. How unfair do you think life is for an Autistic or disabled person? What, if anything, can people who care do to make the situation better?
2. Do you think the rules your culture has for how people think and act make people think Autism and Autistic people are bad? Tell us about that.
3. Are there laws in your country that are unfair to Autistic people? Tell us about that.
4. Have you, or someone you know, been through a dangerous situation with the police because the officer(s) don't understand Autism?
5. As an Autistic person, do you think you are an inspiration for non-Autistic people? Why or why not?
6. Do you think you inspire your Autistic peers? Are there any Autistics who inspire you?
7. What are some ways you find helpful to learn about your rights and how to protect them as an Autistic youth or young adult?
8. What is the best way for everyone to learn about Autism and neurodiversity?

Appendix B

Respondent Information/ Contacts

Below is a list of contributors to this book. This is not a comprehensive list, as many contributors asked to remain anonymous. The list reflects anyone who contributed content and was either quoted directly or submitted content that was consulted, summarized, and/or referenced by the authors, *and* who expressed consent to be listed here. Some contributors also provided links to websites, social media, and contact information.

Sue Abramowski

Emmanuel Abua

Jess Baik: @jessbaik

Adeline Balfour

Elise Barnes

Keegan Beecher

Mordi Benhamou: www.amazon.com/Autism-Falafel-Rock-Roll-atypical-ebook/dp/B089ZZMMGM

HG Bidon

Nera Birch: https://theautisticpinup.com; podcast: *I'm Not Drunk, I'm Autistic*: https://anchor.fm/nera-birch

Kate Blackham

Sarah Boon: https://autistcallysarah.com and @saraheboon on Facebook, X, Instagram, and TikTok

Bridge

Ernesto Brunton: @ernestobrunton

Andy Buchanan: www.facebook.com/AndysSpectrum

Siyu (Suzanna) Chen: Instagram: @suzannachen8; https://squarepeg.community/60-s5-ep5-autism-and-the-intersection-of-culture-race-and-gender

Chloe: https://twitter.com/truthautistic; www.facebook.com/AutisticTruth

Marcelle Ciampi: www.linkedin.com/in/marcelle-ciampi-samantha-craft-290a11b6

Kate Cleaver: https://katemurray.co.uk

Tracey Cohen: www.growingupautistic.com/tracey.html

Alan Conrad

Ty Cordeiro: @tycordeiro; linktree: tycordeiro

Nicole Corrado: www.nicolecorradoart.wordpress.com

Day

Matt Dunford: www.facebook.com/mattdunford; www.instagram.com/mattdunford; www.linkedin.com/in/mattdunford

Emily: @21andsensory; https://21andsensory.wordpress.com; podcast: https://plinkhq.com/i/1271503548

Eric Evans: @przm.sensory, @Konafocust3; www.facebook.com/XLR8.BOLT

Ezra

Yelena Forrester

Billie-Jade Fox: www.girlonthespectrumcom.wordpress.com

Michael Fugate: www.alignable.com/fort-wayne-in/michael-fugate-advocate-for-the-disabled

Alexa Gallant: https://alexagallant.com

Mikan Gensic

Medusa (Lucy Hall)

Emma Harrington: @EmmaliaWrites

Freddy Henderson: https://i-dont-look-autistic.com

Kristen Hovet: @otherautismpodcast

Robbie Ierubino: www.ierubino.com, Instagram, LinkedIn, X, YouTube

Jeremiah Josey

Brianna Kimble: @service.doodle.piper

Ettina Kitten

Kmarie: http://worldwecreate.blogspot.com

Tas Kronby: https://tasthewriter.com

Lucas Ksenhuk

Sarah L.

Madison Lessard: @madisonlessard

Grace Liu: book: *Approaching Autistic Adulthood: The Road Less Travelled*; blog: https://unwrittengrace.wordpress.com; website: https://artistic-autistic.co.uk; Facebook: www.facebook.com/unwrittengrace; Instagram: @unwrittengraceblogs

Lucy M.: https://amythicalcreature.wordpress.com; X: https://twitter.com/hydrogenjukebox

Mike Macedo

Kerrin Maclean: Instagram: @aspieanswers; X: @Aspie Answers; YouTube: www.youtube.com/c/AspieAnswers; website: www.aspieanswers.com

Nicnac Marsh: podcast: *The Nicnac Podcast: Conversations About Divergent Life*

Hanna Mashima: https://linktr.ee/hannamashima

Flo Neville: florenceneville.com

Stephen McHugh: https://stephensevolution.com

Olivia Nied: www.olivianied.com

Noor: www.instagram.com/muslimmamaonthespectrum

Nora

ChrisTiana ObeySumner: www.christianaobeysumner.com; LinkedIn: www.Linkedin.com/in/ChrisTianaObeySumner

JJ Oesterle: Facebook

Logan P.

Max Pavlak

Skye Perryn

Julianna Phillips

Yenn Purkis/Tanya Masterman: www.yennpurkis.com

Raj

Khali Raymond: www.khaliraymond.com

Tejas Rayo Sankar: www.crimsonrise.org; @tejasraosankar

Sarah Reade: https://toaspieornottoaspie.com

Emma Reardon: www.autismwellbeing.org.uk

Alice Running

Sarah

Rakshita Shekhar

Molly Smith: https://mollysmusingsonlife.wordpress.com

Leigh Spence: X and YouTube: *One Awesome Autistic*

Ceaser Stringfield

Teona Studemire: @teonawrites for all social media handles

Gregory Tino: *The Autistic Mind Finally Speaks*: https://inautism.wordpress.com

Michele Truty: https://delightfullyquirky.me; @delightfully_quirky

Marley Vaughan: Instagram: @marleyvaughann

Lyndon Voss: *An AgVoss Public Service Announcement*: https://youtu.be/kfbJTajmadE

Ken Vu: Instagram and TikTok: @theautismexperience; podcast: *The Autism Experience*

Michael Gerard Walzer: www.thehiddengiftsproject.com

Laura Weldon ND, MS: www.weldonwellness.com; Instagram: @neurodivergent.naturopath

Daniel Williams: https://m.facebook.com/williams.daniel3

Morgan Young

References

Amplifier (n.d.). Amplifier Art Amplifies Movements. Amplifier. Retrieved June 2, 2023, from https://amplifier.org.

Autistic Self Advocacy Network. (n.d.). *Civic Engagement Toolbox for Self-Advocates*. ASAN. Retrieved June 2, 2023, from https://autisticadvocacy.org/policy/toolkits/civic.

Autistic Self Advocacy Network. (n.d.). *Getting and Advocating for Community-Based Housing*. ASAN. Retrieved June 2, 2023, from https://autisticadvocacy.org/wp-content/uploads/2016/12/FND-community-based-housing-non-FL.pdf.

Autistic Self Advocacy Network. (n.d.). *The Right to Make Choices: International Laws and Decision-Making by People with Disabilities*. ASAN. Retrieved June 2, 2023, from https://autisticadvocacy.org/policy/toolkits/choices/#:~:text=The toolkit is called "The,the right to manage their.

Autistic Self Advocacy Network. (n.d.). *The Transition to Adulthood for Youth with I/DD: A Review of Research, Policy and Next Steps*. ASAN. Retrieved June 2, 2023, from https://autisticadvocacy.org/policy/briefs/healthcare-transition.

Autistic Self Advocacy Network. (n.d.). *What is Police Violence?* ASAN. Retrieved June 2, 2023, from https://autisticadvocacy.org/policy/toolkits/police.

Autistic Self Advocacy Network. (2013, July 26). *Empowering Leadership: A Systems Change Guide for Autistic College Students and Those with Other Disabilities*. ASAN. Retrieved June 2, 2023, from https://autisticadvocacy.org/book/empowering-leadership-a-systems-change-guide-for-autistic-college-students-and-those-with-other-disabilities.

Autistic Self Advocacy Network. (2013, July 26). *Navigating College: A Handbook on Self Advocacy*. ASAN. Retrieved June 2, 2023, from https://autisticadvocacy.org/book/navigating-college.

Autistic Self Advocacy Network. (2016, November 14). *Roadmap to Transition: A Handbook for Autistic Youth Transitioning to Adulthood*. ASAN. Retrieved June 2, 2023, from https://autisticadvocacy.org/book/roadmap.

Autistic Self Advocacy Network and Autism Now Center. (n.d.). *Accessing Home and Community-Based Services: A Guide for Self-Advocates*. Retrieved June 2, 2023, from https://autisticadvocacy.org/book/accessing-hcbs.

Barnes, R. (2022, February 8). *"No you're not"—a portrait of autistic women*. Wellcome Collection. Retrieved June 2, 2023, from https://wellcomecollection.org/articles/Yd8L-hAAAIAWFxqa.

Brunton, J. (2022). *Please stop calling autism a disease*. Full Spectrum Mama. Retrieved June 2, 2023, from http://fullspectrummama.blogspot.com/2022/10/a-series-of-humble-requests-3-please.html.

Centers for Disease Control and Prevention. (2023, May 15). "Disability Impacts All of Us" Infographic. Centers for Disease Control and Prevention. Retrieved June 2, 2023, from www.cdc.gov/ncbddd/disabilityandhealth/infographic-disability-impacts-all.html.

Chen, G. (2022, November 28). *Should Public Schools Provide Students with Vocational Opportunities?* Public School Review. Retrieved June 2, 2023, from www.publicschoolreview.com/blog/should-public-schools-provide-students-with-vocational-opportunities.

Curry, A.E. (2021, January 28). *Young Autistic Drivers Crash Less Than Their Non-Autistic Peers*. Center for Injury Research and Prevention (CIRP). Retrieved June 2, 2023, from https://injury.research.chop.edu/blog/posts/young-autistic-drivers-crash-less-than-their-non-autistic-peers

Detester Magazine & Chen, S. (n.d.). *A Guide to Identifying True Autism Advocacy Organizations*. Retrieved September 19, 2023, from https://docs.google.com/document/d/1mSHw8kdHyDH3UfJq8fwu7SC_YCz56Z-jufigJi-pchgo.

Detester Magazine & Chen, S. (n.d.). *Resources for Autistic People*. Retrieved September 19, 2023, from https://docs.google.com/document/d/1QCszd8AJcEs1ou-Hcryj4Q_cKT8xsvF3HQL6vto8lto.

Gopalan, A. (2023, March 29). *Jorts The Cat Wants You To Fight Back*. In These Times. Retrieved June 2, 2023, from https://inthesetimes.com/article/jorts-the-cat-wants-you-to-fight-back.

Guy, Z. (2021, September 1). *Activist Lydia X. Z. Brown Talks Disability Justice, Mutual Aid, and More*. Marie Claire. Retrieved June 2, 2023, from www.marieclaire.com/politics/a35866693/lydia-x-z-brown-interview-2021.

Kiefer, J. (2022, April 19). *"We Are Different": What Black Communities Can Teach Doctors and Scientists*. University of Utah Health Sciences. Retrieved June 2, 2023, from https://uofuhealth.utah.edu/newsroom/news/2022/04/autism-black-parents.

Ladau, E. (2021). *Demystifying Disability: What to Know, What to Say, and How to be an Ally*. New York, NY: Random House.

Lakhiani, V. (2019). *The Code of the Extraordinary Mind*. Penguin Random House. Retrieved June 2, 2023, from www.penguinrandomhouse.com/books/593005/the-code-of-the-extraordinary-mind-by-vishen-lakhiani-founder-of-mindvalley.

Mandell, D.S., Wiggins, L.D., Carpenter, L.A., Daniels, J. *et al.* (2009, March). Racial/ethnic disparities in the identification of children with autism spectrum disorders. *American Journal of Public Health*, 99(3), 493–498. 10.2105/AJPH.2007.131243

Milton, D. (2018, March 2). *The Double Empathy Problem*. National Autistic Society. Retrieved June 2, 2023, from www.autism.org.uk/advice-and-guidance/professional-practice/double-empathy.

Pulrang, A. (2019). *How to Avoid "Inspiration Porn."* Forbes.com. Retrieved June 2, 2023, from www.forbes.com/sites/andrewpulrang/2019/11/29/how-to-avoid-inspiration-porn/?sh=60a848725b3d.

Purkis, Y. & Masterman, T. (2020). *The Awesome Autistic Go-To Guide: A Practical Handbook for Autistic Teens and Tweens*. London: Jessica Kingsley Publishing.

Rodriguez, O. (2022, June 6). *Medical Biases Keep LGBTQ+ BIPOC from Seeking ADHD and Autism Care*. Prism Reports. Retrieved June 2, 2023, from https://prismreports.org/2022/06/06/medical-biases-keep-lgbtq-bipoc-from-seeking-adhd-and-autism-care.

Wong, A. (ed.) (2020). *Disability Visibility: Twenty-First Century Disabled Voices*. New York, NY: Vintage Books.

World Health Organization. (2023, March 7). *Disability*. World Health Organization (WHO). Retrieved June 2, 2023, from www.who.int/news-room/fact-sheets/detail/disability-and-health.